"Why didn't you ever get married, Caroline?"

It was the last thing she'd expected Sloan to ask. She tried to laugh off the question. "Now you sound like my mother."

"But why didn't you?" he pressed. "You're great with kids, you've got a great sense of humor—"

Caroline shuddered. "And a terrific personality, yes, I know. That's the absolute kiss of death for a woman." She shook her head, wishing she could ignore the effects of Sloan's touch as easily. She could still feel his fingertips brushing along her face.

She could tell he was waiting for her to say more. "I guess I've just been too busy." She looked away. "Maybe I just never met the right person."

"No one? In all this time?"

"There was someone," she said quietly, unable to help herself. "But he was already taken."

Dear Reader,

Once again, Intimate Moments offers you top-notch romantic reading, with six more great books from six more great authors. First up is *Gage Butler's Reckoning,* the latest in Justine Davis's TRINITY STREET WEST miniseries. It seems Gage has a past, a past that includes a girl—now a woman—with reason to both hate him and love him. And his past is just about to become his present.

Maria Ferrarella's *A Husband Waiting To Happen* is a story of second chances that will make you smile, while Maura Seger's *Possession* is a tale of revenge and matrimony that will have you longing for a cooling breeze—even if it *is* only March! You'll notice our new Conveniently Wed flash on Kayla Daniels' *Her First Mother.* We'll be putting this flash on more marriage of convenience books in the future, but this is a wonderful and emotional way to begin. Another flash, The Loving Arms of the Law, has been chosen to signify novels featuring sheriffs, those perfect Western heroes. And Kay David's *Lone-Star Lawman* is an equally perfect introduction. Finally, enjoy *Montoya's Heart,* Bonnie Gardner's second novel, following her successful debut, *Stranger In Her Bed.*

And, of course, don't forget to come back next month, when we'll have six more Intimate Moments novels guaranteed to sweep you away into a world of excitement and passion.

Enjoy!

Leslie J. Wainger
Senior Editor and Editorial Coordinator

Please address questions and book requests to:
Silhouette Reader Service
U.S.: 3010 Walden Ave., P.O. Box 1325, Buffalo, NY 14269
Canadian: P.O. Box 609, Fort Erie, Ont. L2A 5X3

MARIE FERRARELLA

A HUSBAND WAITING TO HAPPEN

Silhouette®
INTIMATE™ MOMENTS®

Published by Silhouette Books

America's Publisher of Contemporary Romance

SILHOUETTE BOOKS

ISBN 0-373-07842-0

A HUSBAND WAITING TO HAPPEN

Copyright © 1998 by Marie Rydzynski-Ferrarella

Printed in U.S.A.

MARIE FERRARELLA

lives in southern California. She describes herself as the tired mother of two overenergetic children and the contented wife of one wonderful man. This RITA Award-winning author is thrilled to be following her dream of writing full-time.

In memory of
Erika Wolff,
my other mother.
Your children miss you, Mom.

Chapter 1

"Mr. Walters, if you've got a minute, I'd like you to listen to something."

Ambushed outside his classroom and a good twenty feet shy of the exit, Sloan Walters temporarily aborted his escape to freedom. He glanced at his watch. Almost four o'clock. He was supposed to have been in the parking lot getting into his car over an hour ago. Somehow, the past sixty-eight minutes had managed to completely slip away, without his being conscious of it.

So what else was new? Students always seemed to materialize out of nowhere with problems just as he was about to leave for the day. And it never happened more frequently than when he was in a hurry. That, too, was nothing new.

He'd never developed the knack of saying no to an earnest student. It was one of the things that made him so popular at Bedford High. Students clamored to sign up for his classes, both the ones he'd had to take over

in drama and his own English classes. They were drawn
to his classes by his energy, his honesty and, where most
of his female students were concerned, by his rugged,
almost brooding dark blond good looks. The last group
came for the view and stayed for the education. Everyone agreed that Sloan Walters had the ability to breathe
life into the dullest, driest of topics. It was a gift he
seemed to be singularly unaware of.

But everyone else was aware of it. Students sought
him out as a mentor and as a counselor, trusting him
with their problems, their secret hopes and fears, the way
they would no one else. He was genuinely flattered by
their trust, and while he valued the esteem the students
rendered him, there were times when being the one they
turned to got in the way of his personal life.

Like now. Trying not to appear impatient, Sloan
shifted his briefcase to his other hand. "Okay, but this
is *really* going to have to take only a minute, Allison.
I'm running late."

Eager to please, Allison McGeever gave a quick nod.
Without another unnecessary word, she launched into a
single rousing and melodic chorus of "You Can't Get a
Man with a Gun." Never mind that they were in the
middle of the hallway, between the student lockers and
the administration office. She gave it her all. Allison
sang for him the way she had for her mirror, the way
she intended to for the audience who would eventually
fill the seats of the auditorium where the annual spring
play was going to be held.

By the time the last note of the chosen chorus was
echoing down the hallway, both the secretary and the
vice principal had poked their heads out of the administration office, curious to discover what was going on
and who was singing so loudly after school hours. They

remained to form a silent, appreciative audience, and applauded with feeling once Allison was finished.

But there was only one opinion that mattered to her. Allison bit her lower lip and looked hopefully at the teacher all her girlfriends referred to as "the hunk" behind his back. Mr. Walters was always kind, even in his criticism, but she was after praise. It had been his criticism at last night's rehearsal that sent her to her bedroom and to endless hours of practice.

"More authoritative?"

Sloan smiled, pleased by the effort he'd witnessed. He'd known she had it in her when he made his appraisal last night.

"Much." So saying, he began to back away, casting an eye toward the door and his goal.

Allison flushed with pleasure. She matched his steps, reluctant to lose his company.

"That was the word you used," she reminded him as Sloan placed his hand against the front door and began to push it open. "Authoritative. You said I should be more authoritative as Annie. I've been practicing," she called after him as he stepped over the threshold.

The difference between her almost mundane rendition of the same song last night and today's energetic sampling was tremendous. Allison had obviously put in a lot of work, he thought. That was what he liked best about dealing with students—the effort they put out in perfecting something that was important to them. Here, in a relatively well-off and sheltered community, they were all still too young to realize that no matter what they did, life had already stacked the deck against them.

Just as he hadn't known at their age.

But he did now.

There was no reason to share this piece of information

with them. They'd discover it on their own soon enough. For now, there were illusions for them to polish. And, as they polished them, sometimes he even got caught up in them himself.

"And it shows. Keep up the good work." Sloan waved a hand at the girl in his wake. "See you at rehearsal tomorrow."

It was a general, throwaway comment, but she clung to it and filled it with all sorts of hidden meanings and innuendos. Allison smiled giddily, hugging her books to her chest.

"I'll be there," she promised, raising her voice so that it would carry to him as the door closed behind Sloan.

Since she was his leading lady in *Annie Get Your Gun*, the musical he'd been tapped to direct this year for Bedford High School, he certainly hoped she would be there, Sloan thought with a soundless laugh.

Hurrying down the flight of cement steps leading to the parking lot, Sloan felt his pockets for his keys.

And now, he mused as he searched for the key that fit into the door of his '83 Mazda, he needed not to be here, but somewhere else. Opening the door on the driver's side, he tossed his briefcase onto the passenger seat, then got in and started the car.

Sloan pulled out and merged into light traffic. Actually, he needed to be in two places at once. Home and school. He blew out a breath as the light at the end of the block turned red. He was probably going to catch every one. It figured. It always seemed to be that way these days. There was never enough time to do everything. Never enough time to do his job right and still not shortchange his sons.

There might be time, he reminded himself, if he hadn't been maneuvered into volunteering to take on this year's play. But Mrs. Jacobs, who usually handled the job of directing, was out on maternity leave, and he had been the next logical choice. So, he had said yes, adding this to the ever-growing list of things that required his attention. Now, with rehearsals and the myriad of details that went along with putting on the school play, he had absolutely no time for a life of his own. Outside of caring for the boys, of course.

Danny and Joey always came first, even though at times, he knew, it didn't seem that way to them. In order to give them the time they deserved, Sloan had trained himself to require only five hours of sleep a night. Six, if he was feeling particularly decadent. Even so, his life was filled to the brim, with no space left over for anything that didn't involve his family or the school.

And that was just the way he wanted it, Sloan thought. He didn't need time to socialize. Not the way he used to. Where once he'd loved surrounding himself with the boisterous company of others, there seemed to be no reason for it anymore. Not without Ju—

Sloan simultaneously slammed down on his thoughts and on the brake just as he came to the corner. Exhaling slowly, grateful that he hadn't caused an accident, he turned right.

The memories had almost managed to break through that time, moving stealthily toward him in the dark, like a sniper with a high-powered rifle. Ready to blow him apart. But he wouldn't allow it. Wouldn't allow the thought of Julie to haunt him.

He was only half-conscious of the small sigh escaping his lips. Sloan was far more aware of barring the very thought's existence, and with it, the emotion that was attached to it. Barring it just the way he'd been doing for the past year.

The past thirteen months.

He didn't want thoughts of Julie crowding his mind. There was no point in it. Julie was gone, and she wasn't coming back. Thinking about her wasn't going to change anything, or make it any easier on him. It would do just the opposite. He was fine as long as he kept moving, kept busy. As long as he kept filling his mind with things that needed doing, until there was no leftover space for anything else.

For anyone else.

And if there was no place for the thought, for the memory that had been his wife, there would be no place for the pain, either. The excruciating pain that could so very easily rob him of the ability to even breathe. It could certainly rob him of the ability to function. He knew that firsthand. He'd made the mistake of letting the memories come just once. The accompanying pain had paralyzed him, almost completely destroyed him.

If that had happened, where would his sons be?

His sons were both so young, so in need of someone to watch over them. They needed him. Sure, there was his mother, but she had a life of her own, and besides, Danny and Joey needed a parent in their lives. At least one. They had a right to that.

For better or worse, he was it.

He was getting better at that job all the time, Sloan told himself as guilt over running late nibbled away at him. He was a lot better at it now than he had been a year ago. Life had forced on him a lot of hands-on experience since Julie's death, and he'd conquered things he'd never dreamed of doing. Like writing up tightly knit schedules, and doing laundry in the middle of the night.

Now if he could only learn how to cook, he thought philosophically, he'd be perfect.

Cook.

A sinking feeling torpedoed his stomach.

He was supposed to have picked up three microwave dinners on his way home. His mother wasn't staying for dinner tonight, which meant that he and the boys would have to fend for themselves. And that, in turn, meant dinners that required thawing and that came from the supermarket.

The supermarket he had just passed.

Biting off a few choice words regarding the chaotic state of his mind and his forgetfulness these days, Sloan glanced in his rearview mirror. Clear. Holding his breath, he executed a sharp slide to the left, getting into the turn lane just as the traffic light hanging over it turned green. Coming out of the slide, he did a U-turn he would have been proud of ten years ago.

Ten years ago he wouldn't have kept one eye out for the police, either, he thought. But time, necessity and fatherhood had taught him to be more cautious than the high-spirited youth he'd once been.

High-spirited? Sloan shook his head as he guided his car into the parking lot. He'd been a hell-raiser, pure and simple. It was one of the things that had attracted the girls to him. He'd smelled of danger, or so he had liked to think back then. He'd known the girls thought so. His buddies had all told him.

Not that he'd really noticed that much. Even back then, his heart had already been sewn up.

Damn, he was letting it happen again.

Getting out of the car, Sloan slammed the door shut behind him. What the hell was wrong with him today, anyway? Was it the smell of spring in the air that was doing this to him? Ambushing him, firing arrows tipped with memories in his direction?

That had to be it. Spring. Spring was when they had started going together. It had been spring the very first time they had made love. And spring when he had asked her to marry him.

Spring should be banned, he thought cynically as he marched into the supermarket.

The doors barely had enough time to pull open for him before he was crossing the threshold.

Sloan commandeered a steel shopping cart and aimed it like a weapon at the middle of the store, where the frozen foods were kept.

With the discipline of the athlete he'd once been, Sloan concentrated on the time, and nothing else. His mother had a party to go to tonight. She'd told him in no uncertain terms that she couldn't watch the boys after four-thirty. Without looking at his watch, he knew there was less than half an hour's grace period left. He also knew his mother would cut him a little slack if he was late, but not much. She was adamant about being on time. He had to hurry.

Selecting three dinners at random, feeling no particular enthusiasm for any of them, Sloan smiled wryly. Who would have ever thought? These days, his mother had a far more thriving social life than he did. The tables had certainly turned. Now he was the one who sat at home, telling her to be careful as she went gallivanting off into the night with her friends.

But he was glad for her, glad to see his mother grabbing life with both hands and enjoying herself. Even if it did cut holes in the time she normally reserved for caring for his sons.

Things could always be worked out. If tonight was a

rehearsal night, he would have taken the boys with him. They were young enough not to complain about being dragged around by their father. At six and eight, it was still fun and a big deal for them to "see where Dad works." And if sometimes it hurt to look into their faces and see so much of Julie there, well, it was a bittersweet pain. One that he had learned to live with.

Not like the other.

Damn it.

Impatient with himself and the lack of control he seemed to have over his own mind tonight, Sloan muttered a curse as he turned the corner sharply. He shoved the cart in front of him.

And right into the cart that had chosen that moment to occupy the space he was aiming for. The resounding clatter of metal hitting metal sent vibrations running through him.

Chagrined, Sloan looked up at the woman, an apology forming in his mouth. It evaporated before it fully emerged.

"I'm very sor— Caroline?" Surprised, Sloan stared at the dark-haired woman on the receiving end of the collision.

Recognition was immediate, bringing Caroline Masters out of her mental fog as quickly as the snap of a hypnotist's fingers lifted a spell. Immediate, too, was the short, strong flutter in the pit of her stomach, like the engine of a plane starting up.

For exactly one second, she was transported back in time. She was fifteen again, and achingly in love with Sloan Walters.

Achingly and silently. Because Julie was in love with him, too, and Julie Simone was the dearest friend she had in the world.

Caroline prayed that the flush she felt creeping up her neck was the work of her imagination and nothing more. She was Dr. Masters now, and doctors weren't supposed to blush like untried pubescent virgins. Never mind that two-thirds of that description was still true; she didn't want to look like one.

"The very same," she replied cheerfully. Striving to recover, Caroline glanced at the cart butted up against hers. "I see you still drive with the same wild abandonment you did ten years ago."

The moment the words were out of her mouth, she regretted them. That was how Julie had died, the victim of a reckless, impatient commuter jumping the light because he was late for work. Jumping it and plowing his car straight into Julie's. She'd died instantly.

Foot-in-mouth disease again, Masters, Caroline silently upbraided herself.

But if the comment jarred loose a chain of painful recollections, Sloan didn't show it. Instead, he continued looking at her as he worked the carts loose. She couldn't read his expression.

"What are you doing in town?"

She was the last person he'd expected to bump into like this. The last time he saw Caroline had been just over a year ago. At his wife's funeral. They had comforted each other then. Mostly, Sloan recalled, he had comforted Caroline. He hadn't allowed anyone in to really comfort him. Hadn't let the emotions out where they could destroy him. As long as they were contained, he could keep going. Keep from breaking apart into a thousand, tiny splintered pieces.

So he just kept going, pedaling as fast as he could, always one rotation ahead of the pain.

"Shopping for food," she answered lightly. Her parents' refrigerator was almost empty, a silent testament to just how unraveled her mother had become these past few weeks. Caroline had taken a temporary leave of absence from the clinic where she worked in Albuquerque to try to help. One look at her mother when she arrived had told Caroline that eating regularly had become a low priority for Wanda Masters.

"I see that." Her cart was completely full. The sight of it reminded him of the year before graduation, when he had worked as a box boy. Caroline had done the family shopping at his store every Friday afternoon, after school let out. "Planning on staying awhile?"

She'd made that decision before putting in for her leave. "As a matter of fact, I am."

Caroline debated telling him just what had brought her back. But the explanation required more than just a sentence or two exchanged in the middle of a supermarket. Besides, the mere mention of the reason distressed and embarrassed her mother. It would her father, too, if he was really aware of it.

So Caroline let it go. Sloan didn't need to hear her problems. God knew, he was probably still dealing with enough himself.

Sloan turned his cart toward the front of the store and the checkout counters. Caroline fell into step beside him. "When did you get in?" he asked her.

He expected her to say that she'd arrived just a few hours ago. When she told him it had been a couple of days, it caught him by surprise.

"You've been back more than twenty-four hours and you didn't bother to call?" It wasn't like Caroline not to let him know she was in town. She had always called in the past. He wondered if anything was wrong. Now that he really looked, she did seem a little flushed.

"It's a little complicated," she confessed. "This isn't just a run-of-the-mill visit." Caroline curbed the need to share her reason with someone. "So, how have you been?"

She changed course so quickly, it took Sloan a moment to absorb the question.

"Fine." It was his standard, automatic answer to everyone. Even to himself. He was doing fine, just fine.

The word assaulted her. Sloan had said it too quickly, Caroline thought. Like a pat answer, rendered without thought, to keep people from delving into a sensitive area.

The look in Sloan's eyes reinforced her feelings. He was still hurting, even though she knew he never mentioned it. Never talked about how he felt. It took very little imagination to realize how strongly the pain had settled around his heart.

You'd never know it by the way he acted, though, she thought. The face he turned to the world, even right after the funeral, had always been one of strength and composure. As if to deny the fact that by a stranger's reckless act, his entire world had been blown to smithereens.

No one knew better than she just how much he had loved Julie. She'd been home, on a visit, and with Sloan when he got the telephone call about Julie's accident. In that one moment, when he hung up the receiver, he had looked completely lost, shattered. And then, as if by magic, that look had been erased as Sloan took control over himself.

In the weeks that immediately followed the accident, whenever she tried to offer any words of condolence, Sloan had cut her off, turning the conversation to other things. He wouldn't allow her to help him. Wouldn't allow anyone to help.

As they queued up to the counter, Caroline nodded at his cart. "Don't believe in buying much, do you?"

The boyish grin that had first caught her heart slipped over his lips.

"I just stopped in to pick up dinner for the boys and me. My mother is off to a party," he explained as an afterthought. "She's turned into a regular social butterfly these last few months."

"And you still haven't learned to cook." It wasn't a question. Sloan's range of experience had never carried him toward the kitchen. Why should it? He'd always been surrounded by women ready and willing to do anything that needed doing for him. The amazing thing was that he had never abused that advantage.

Sloan laughed, thinking of the hopeless look on Danny's face last weekend, when he had experimented with making stew. The result had been inedible, and had signaled the termination of one heretofore perfectly good pot. A pot whose bottom had become eternally scarred with charred chunks of beef. No amount of cleaning or elbow grease could dissolve the union. The stew and the pot had suffered the same fate, and ended up in the garbage can. Not even a scavenging neighbor's dog had wanted any part of it.

"No, I guess I still haven't gotten the hang of it. Besides—" he shrugged "—I haven't had the time."

She was well acquainted with that problem. Time was the most precious of commodities when you were a medical student. Her first year, she had averaged just over three hours of sleep a night—when she was lucky.

Caroline smiled fondly. "Been busy?"

Sloan deposited all three dinners on the conveyor belt. "Extremely."

And she had a feeling that in his case, it was more

than just a matter of life sliding downhill on a runaway toboggan. If Sloan didn't have any extra time, it was on purpose. So that he wouldn't have to think. Or to feel.

If she knew Sloan, he was treating grief as if it were the enemy. That meant keeping it at bay.

She wondered just what kind of a toll that had exacted on him. He looked tired.

She began emptying her cart. "You sound like you and the boys could use a home-cooked meal."

He raised a brow. "You offering?"

Cooking relaxed her. These days, puttering around in the kitchen was a treat. "Any time." She lifted four plastic bags of fruit onto the conveyor belt. "I'm here for a month." That should be all the time that was needed.

She thought of her parents. It would be good for both of them to be in a familiar, relaxed situation. Their acquaintance with Sloan went back to her first year in high school. But her mother's wishes took precedence over any good intentions Caroline had. For the time being, she would give them the privacy they wanted. Which meant that Sloan and his sons couldn't come over.

Caroline slanted a look toward him. "The only condition is that it has to be at your house."

He thought that rather an odd stipulation, and was about to ask why when he stopped himself. If she wanted him to know, she'd tell him.

"Sounds fair enough. How about tomorrow night?" His mother was going away for several days to Las Vegas with a busload of her friends, and he and the boys would be on their own again. Takeout was beginning to wear a little thin—although if Joey had his way, all his meals would come wrapped in a white-and-red paper bag, with tiny servings of ketchup on the side.

Tomorrow night. She'd like that, she thought. Seeing his sons again, and cooking for all of them. Caroline grinned as the checker finished ringing him up. "You're on."

Chapter 2

"How did you let these get into such a mess, Mom? Some of these are two months overdue."

Caroline held up a handful of bills to reinforce her point. She'd come into the den on a whim, fueled by an emotional need to return, just for a few moments, to a far less complex time in her life. Caroline could remember sitting here on the floor beside the desk, playing quietly—or a young child's version of quietly—as her father did his work. She must have been no older than six at the time. Her father had smoked a pipe back then, before tobacco received a black name and her mother put her foot down. The smell of cherrywood still made her nostalgic.

It had been when she sat down at the desk that the nostalgic trip abruptly ended. There had been windowed envelopes scattered haphazardly about the desk. More than half had been unopened. The words *Second Notice*, stamped across several, had immediately caught her attention.

Eschewing niceties, she opened one envelope, and then another and another. They were all for bills that remained unpaid. Some had finance charges accruing.

A dull headache was wandering over her brow by the time she finished sorting through them. That was when she called her mother into the room.

Wanda raised her chin defensively in reply to the question.

"I didn't let them get in a mess." She paused, and then the helplessness found her. The helplessness that had haunted her ever since she began to notice her husband's lapses. "Your father did."

Caroline tried not to sound as irritated as she felt. Her mother's reluctance to be held accountable for things wasn't anything new. But this was serious.

"Mother, you know as well as I do that he's been letting things slip by him. You were the one who told me. You should have at least made sure that he was keeping up with all the bills." She glanced at the notice from the mortgage company. They were tersely informing her parents that it had been almost three months since any payment was received from them.

Wanda shook her head. "I can't look over his shoulder. That would be insulting him. You know what a proud man he is."

Caroline couldn't bring herself to believe that her mother was actually stubbornly clinging to flimsy excuses, not at a time like this. "You didn't have to tell him, Mother—just look at the checkbook."

Crimson streaks spread up along Wanda's neck, reaching to her cheeks. She was trapped, and she knew she was wrong. But she didn't like having to explain herself. It just made everything worse. "How can I look at the checkbook when I don't know where it is?"

Caroline stared at her mother. She'd always known that it was her father who took care of things, but she'd always assumed it was out of habit, rather than some tacit, unspoken mandate. She felt as if she'd been dropped into some simpleminded sitcom from the early sixties. Her mother was an educated woman, for heaven's sake.

Maybe she'd heard wrong. "You don't know where the checkbook is?"

"No." Restless, unable to find a place for herself since she had begun to realize that something was terribly wrong with the man she had loved and depended on for most of her adult life, Wanda rose and paced blindly about the small den, too distraught to focus. She twisted her wedding ring around and around her finger, the way she always did when she was upset.

There were deep marks there, as if the ring had worn into her flesh. Caroline could see them from where she was sitting.

Oh, Mother, she thought in sympathy and despair. *Why didn't you call me sooner?*

"No," Wanda repeated, her shoulders momentarily sagging in defeat, "I don't know where the checkbook is. Just like I don't know where the deed to the house is, or the blue slip for the car."

"Pink," Caroline corrected gently. Her mother looked at her blankly. "The ownership slip for a car is pink."

Wanda threw up her hands, angry at being corrected, at being cornered. Angry at life for pulling the rug out from under her this way.

"Pink, blue, what difference does it make? I wouldn't know any of the papers if I tripped over them." Frustration marred the brow she oh-so-carefully moisturized every night in an attempt to look eternally young for a husband who would love her if she was wrinkled and wizened. "That's always been your father's responsibility, not mine. Not mine," she echoed softly, as if she were saying the words to herself.

Oh, God, where did she begin to unscramble all this? Caroline wondered. A wave of overwhelming despair threatened to soak her through and through, if she would allow it.

The temptation to just take things over, to do, rather than to teach, was enormous. Heaven knew, in the long run, it would be a lot easier for her to do it that way.

But it was the long run that her mother might be faced with, and someone had to show her that she had a backbone, that she could and *would* survive, if she only dug deep into herself and stopped running. Giving in to despair and breaking down wasn't going to help Wanda or her husband. Caroline had to make her understand that.

"Mom." Caroline rose and placed her hands on her mother's shoulders. "You're going to have to be strong."

As if touched by a hot branding iron, Wanda shrugged Caroline's hands off. "I don't have to be anything of the sort. Your father's going to get well. Josh is going to get well," she insisted. "He's always been a strong man. Never sick a day in his life. This is temporary, just temporary."

Her dark eyes were pleading for reassurance when she looked up at Caroline. Whether there was truth behind the words or not was something she'd deal with later. Right now, all she wanted was to be told it was all going to be all right.

So far, from what Caroline had witnessed firsthand

these past couple of days, her father appeared to be only
a little absentminded, nothing more. But it wasn't simple
absentmindedness that had prompted her mother to call
her earlier this week, fear rimming her voice as she
asked her to come home immediately. Some innate sense
had told Caroline that this time, it wasn't just her
mother's tendency to overdramatize; there was something more to it. If she'd had any doubts, the mountain
of unpaid bills went a long way toward dispelling them.
Her father had always prided himself on never being in
debt to anyone. The bills would never have been allowed
to pile up if he was in complete control of his faculties.

Caroline knew where everything was pointing, and
her mother had to be ready for the worst, in case the
worst was what she had to face.

"It might not be temporary," Caroline said gently.
"You have to be prepared for that."

"I don't have to be prepared for anything," Wanda
snapped back.

Caroline sighed. She slipped her arm around her
mother. When had she gotten to feel so fragile? "And
even if it is temporary, you have to be there for him.
The way he's always been here for you."

Desperation mingled with defiance. "I *am* there for
him," Wanda insisted. "I love that man to distraction.
I always have. And when he wakes up at night, maybe
a little afraid, maybe thinking what you're thinking,
reaching for me, for his wife, I'm there. I'm the one who
makes the shadows go away."

It wasn't enough. It might have been under ordinary
circumstances, but it wasn't now. Not if it turned out to
be what she suspected. "There's more to it than just
being a night-light, Mom." For once in her life, her
mother was going to have to take charge of things. But

Caroline knew it wasn't something that came easily to her. "Just because Grandfather was overbearing and wouldn't let you think for yourself, just because Dad took over everything so you wouldn't be 'bothered' by it, doesn't mean you don't have it in you to handle things."

Pampered all her life, Wanda McKee Masters had never had to do for herself in the real world. The college degree she'd obtained represented knowledge for its own sake. She'd never had to face the mundane, taxing details of an everyday life.

Wanda chewed on her lower lip, worrying it. "But I don't."

"Yes, you do. Balancing a checkbook doesn't take someone who knows Boolean algebra, Mom. It takes someone who knows simple math, that's all. You've organized those parties of yours all these years, you can organize a damn checking account." The pained expression on her mother's face made her realize that she'd raised her voice. "You can," she repeated more softly. "Mom, all your life, everyone's treated you like you were spun out of glass, but you're not."

She could see that she wasn't getting through. Caroline tried again. "You're strong. Some of me must have come from you, and I am not a weak person."

A fond, sad smile curved her mother's mouth. "You're your father's daughter."

Caroline took hold of the hands that had fussed over her when she was young, trying to arrange her hair, to make her look pretty, like the other girls. They'd fussed in vain. She hadn't been like the other girls, she'd been herself. A little withdrawn, a little unconventional, a little restless to find a place for herself where there didn't seem to be any. She'd always walked her own path, and the road hadn't been one her mother wanted to see her on. She had a profession, not a marriage, and patients, not children. But it suited her.

"I am your daughter, too," Caroline said firmly. "And I know you can take charge of your life. Now, whatever is wrong with Dad, temporary or not, we're going to face it together. You and me, understand?" Slowly she stroked away the lines upon the forehead of the face she loved so well. "You and me."

The eyes that looked up at her were unconvinced.

Neither woman realized that they were no longer alone in the den.

"Plotting a conspiracy?" Joshua Masters's laugh boomed, filling the room as he walked in. He moved with certainty, a lion reclaiming his pride. With his flowing mane of white hair and tall, robust stature, he thoroughly looked the part. It was that same bearing that had made people trust him with their dreams when he headed his own construction company. He was the sort of man who could turn dreams into reality.

He sounded so like himself. For a hope-filled moment, Caroline thought that maybe her mother was guilty of blowing things out of proportion. It wouldn't have been the first time Wanda Masters had gotten emotionally carried away. So far, apart from the pile of bills, her father had exhibited no real signs of the vacant meandering her mother had told her about in terrified whispers, as if the sound of the words said out loud would somehow intensify the situation.

She needed more evidence to go on, Caroline thought, one way or another.

But, for now, she played it light. "I'm just trying to educate Mom on the finer points of check writing."

"Now why would you want to do that?" Picking up

one stack of bills as if he'd never seen them before, Josh glanced down at the top one. And then at the one behind it. The smile on his broad face froze a little around the edges and struggled for survival. What remained had lost half its heart.

He looked not unlike a rebellious boy, Caroline thought, who'd been caught forgetting to take out the trash. Again. Joshua Masters dropped the bills on the desktop, pushing the piles together with his large, capable hands.

"I'll get to them. I've been busy. No need to bother your mother with any of that."

Caroline knew that her father meant well, but that was part of the problem. "Mom should know how to—"

The smile returned, full and loving. "Your mother is fine just the way she is. We're both fine just the way we are." The love he felt for his daughter shone in his gray eyes. He hugged her to him with one arm. "Just because you've got that degree of yours, Carrie, doesn't mean you have to start practicing on us." Releasing Caroline, he turned to his wife. "Wanda, where's the aspirin? I've got a headache that's taking the top of my head off."

Pieces were fitting together all too well, even though she didn't want them to. "Do you get these headaches often, Dad?"

Joshua raised a shaggy white eyebrow. "Don't you have a dinner to cook for that friend of yours?" he asked. "How is Sloan doing, anyway?"

Caroline shrugged, for now allowing her father to change the subject. She'd get her answers soon enough. "As well as can be expected, I suppose, and yes, I do have a dinner to cook, so I guess I'd better get going."

She could have sworn her father looked relieved. And then the look evaporated as he smiled fondly at his wife.

"You're going to miss a great dinner here. Your mother's decided to experiment and try something new. Chicken à la king, isn't it, dear?"

Wanda's translucent skin became a shade paler. "Yes, chicken à la king." She shot a furtive glance at Caroline.

Joshua noticed the exchange. Something distant nagged at him, but he couldn't catch it. Impatience, usually so foreign to his makeup, pricked at him. "What?" he asked his wife.

"Nothing, dear," Wanda murmured.

Communication had to start somewhere. They couldn't continue tiptoeing around the subject. Her father couldn't just wander in the dark like this.

Caroline took a deep breath. "Dad, it's your favorite."

Bewilderment met her remark. "What is?"

Caroline could feel her heart constrict a little. "Chicken à la king. It's your favorite dish. Mom's been making it for you for years."

Joshua wanted to deny it. Heatedly. But something told him his daughter was right. He felt like a man under the veil of amnesia, felt as if his life weren't his own anymore. He fought the feeling and denied his blunder.

"Of course it is." He laughed expansively, sweeping his glance from one to the other. "Can't you girls tell when someone's pulling your leg?" Hating what he saw in his daughter's eyes, Josh looked away and planted himself at his desk. "Now go. As you've pointed out, I've got bills to pay, and I can't do it with you two standing around talking."

Caroline wanted to remain, to help, but knew it would only make things worse, so she slipped out behind her mother. Looking over her shoulder, she saw her father sitting at his desk, the way she had seen him hundreds of times before. She clung to the image, but knew it was only that, an image. She couldn't do what her mother had done, couldn't slip into the cushiony realm of denial. She hadn't the luxury.

As soon as the door was closed and they were down the hall, Caroline stopped her mother. No more pussy-footing around. "What kinds of tests has he had?"

Wanda looked at her blankly. "Tests?"

Caroline bit back exasperation. Hadn't they even taken the first logical step? "Tests, Mother. An MRI, blood work, a CAT scan," she enumerated. Caroline knew the answer before it came. "Nothing?"

Wanda lifted her head, trying to hang on to tattered hope. "He keeps saying he's fine."

They both knew he wasn't. And they both knew her mother didn't really believe him when he said he was. If she did, there wouldn't haven't been the telephone call in the dead of night, asking Caroline to come home.

But it wouldn't do any good to keep hammering away at her. Wanda Masters was frightened enough as it was. Caroline slipped her arm around her mother's shoulders again and ushered her into the living room.

"First thing tomorrow, I'll make a few calls. Dr. Wiseman is still his doctor, isn't he?" Her mother nodded. "All right, I'll talk to him. Dad has to have a complete workup."

"Caroline, is that necessary?"

Caroline was trying to keep back her own emotions, the way she'd managed to contain them most of her life. But for a moment, they broke free, spilling out. "Of course it's necessary, Mother. Don't you want to know what you're facing?"

A spark of defiance returned to her mother's eyes.

"No. All I want to know is that Josh is going to get better."

Caroline pressed her lips together. The only scrap of strength and stubbornness her mother displayed, and it had to be misplaced. She felt drained, tired. Maybe she needed to cook this dinner for Sloan and his sons more than they needed to eat it, she thought. She needed to get away and clear her head.

She crossed to the doorway. There were still a few things she wanted to pick up at the market. She doubted she'd find the ingredients in Sloan's kitchen.

"I've got to get going. We'll talk when I get back." And she knew that it was going to be as futile then as it was now, but she'd be better equipped to deal with her mother's fears.

Later, Caroline told herself. She'd think about all this later. Right now, there was a hungry friend waiting for her.

"But why can't we have pizza? We always have pizza when G-mama goes to Vegas." Danny Walters's high voice swelled as he fought the good fight, following his father into the dining room.

Frustrated, he exchanged looks with his younger brother. Joey shrugged, his hands extended, palms up. "Yeah," he piped up, not knowing what else to say.

Danny gave him a disgusted look and took the lead again. He saw that they were losing this battle. Dad was putting dishes out. They always had pizza in the family room, off paper plates and in front of the big-screen TV, not on real plates in the dining room. Why was this time different from the others? His stomach turned over. Dad wasn't going to make something again, was he? He still had a funny taste in his mouth from the last time.

Sloan hadn't realized how much he was looking forward to seeing Caroline until just now, when he saw his reflection in the microwave above the stove. There was a smile on his face. It was nice, seeing someone from the old days, when life hadn't been quite so crazy.

"Tonight, we're having a regular dinner," he told his firstborn. Sloan laid out four plates the way a blackjack dealer dealt cards on a green velvet tabletop.

Joey tugged on his arm. "Three, Daddy, three. Three plates," he informed his father importantly after doing the math in his head twice. "G-mama's not gonna be here. You made a mistake."

Knives and forks followed the plates. He wondered if he should set out spoons. Caroline hadn't said what she was making when she called to confirm the invitation. "No mistake." He turned to look down at Joey. "Caroline is coming for dinner."

Light brown brows, thin as pencil lines on a mirror pulled together as Joey tried to concentrate. "Caroline?" He repeated the name, but couldn't conjure up a face to match.

"Caroline Masters. Dr. Masters," Sloan added, correcting himself. Now that he thought of it, it seemed the most likely profession for Caroline. There was something soothing about her. Patients would have no trouble turning to someone like her in time of need. "She's a friend of mine."

"Doctor?" Joey looked at his father in horror. The only doctor he knew was Dr. Brady. Dr. Brady had a gruff voice, and big hands that hurt when he sat him up on the table with all the white paper on it. He was a million years old, maybe even more. Joey shivered, remembering his last visit. "Does she give shots?"

"Probably." Turning, Sloan noted his son's eyes. If

he opened them any wider, they'd be in danger of falling out. "Don't worry, she's not giving one to you." He laughed. Joey looked unconvinced. Sloan searched for something to set his son at ease. "You remember Caroline, Joey. She sat·right there on the sofa—" he pointed toward the family room "—and held you on her knee. You played with her bracelets and said you liked the way they jingled."

That had been after the funeral. Funny what a man remembered. There weren't many details that had remained with him of that day. It was all just a black whirl. Comforting looks, hands laid on his shoulder in mute support, none of it seeming to be real. Caroline had taken the kids off his hands, seeing to them as he tried to deal with everything else. Insisted on dealing with everything else.

It had been the only thing that held him together that day.

"Oh." The light dawned. Joey's face lit up like a lantern. "I 'member. She smelled good." A guileless smile replaced his puckered frown. He'd liked Caroline. She'd told him and Danny stories and hugged them to make the ache in their tummies go away. The ache that had come when she explained that Mommy still loved them very, very much, but she wasn't going to be coming back anymore. That God needed her now. "She's coming tonight?"

Danny looked contemptuously at his sibling. A year and a half older, he was warier than Joey. Joey was just a baby, anyway.

"Instead of the pizza," Danny said darkly, crossing his arms before his small chest.

Now what? He'd thought Danny would welcome the opportunity to have a really good meal. Sloan's mother was only fair as far as cooking went. It wasn't one of the things that really interested her. If his memory served, Caroline was a whiz in the kitchen.

"We can always have pizza," he informed Danny, going back to the kitchen to collect four glasses. "Caroline said she was going to cook for us."

Danny cocked his dark head. "Why?" he asked suspiciously.

When had Danny grown so distrustful? Sloan wondered. Had his son always been like this and it had just escaped his notice? It felt as if life were just sifting through his fingers, even as he tried to catch it. "Because she's a friend."

That wasn't a reason, Danny thought. "Billy Peterson's my friend. He never cooked for me."

At the end of a day spent dealing with classrooms full of hormonal teenagers, Sloan's patience was in short supply. He hadn't expected this to turn into a debate.

"He's too young to operate the stove," Sloan pointed out evenly. He heard the doorbell and offered up a silent prayer of thanks. Caroline. Right on time, as usual. "Get that, will you?"

Danny remained where he was, stung at being brushed off and annoyed at being deprived of his very favorite meal in the whole world.

"I'll get it," Joey sang out. He crossed to the front door in a flash, rushing to answer it before his brother had a change of heart. He liked being first—it made him feel important. Yanking the door open, he looked up at Caroline with a bright smile.

Julie's smile, Caroline thought with an unexpected pang. She remembered that exact same smile flashing at her across the playground when they were no more than five years old. Julie had already been a beauty.

Caroline tucked the memory away, then primly looked down into the little boy's face.

"Excuse me, I was looking for the Walters residence, but I must have the wrong house."

Joey grabbed her by the arm before she could get away. He tugged her across the threshold. "No, you don't. This is us."

Caroline bit her tongue to keep from laughing. He looked so very earnest. "Well, you can't be Joey."

He looked down at himself and then back up at her. Confusion highlighted his face. "Why not?"

Someday, she wanted a little boy just like him. It took all she had not to hug Joey to her. "Because you're a young man. The Joey Walters I know is a little boy."

"I grewed," Joey crowed proudly. He threw back his shoulders, confident that it made him at least an inch taller. Maybe more.

Unable to resist, she ruffled his head. He giggled in response. "You certainly did."

Wanting to return the compliment, Joey rose on his toes and took a deep, appreciative breath. "You still smell good."

She inclined her head in a little bow. "Thank you. I try." In the background, she saw another child, a solemn-faced, lanky boy. While Joey had only her smile, Danny had Julie's face. Caroline thought how that had to comfort Sloan, to see a piece of Julie growing this way. She held out her hand to him. "Hello, Danny."

"Hello." His voice was sullen, and he made no attempt to come any closer. Caroline tactfully dropped her hand.

Joey fell into the role of peacemaker naturally. "Danny's mad cause Daddy said we're having you 'steada pizza."

The flicker in Danny's eyes told her Joey was right. She didn't want to make waves. "I see. Well, we can have pizza, too. That way, you can have a choice."

Danny looked at her uncertainly, a hint of a smile playing hide-and-seek on his lips.

Sloan strode into the living room, wiping his hands. He flashed a smile at Caroline. "Don't spoil them any more than they already are."

Caroline tried not to notice that the sight of his smile still did funny things to her insides. Some things, she supposed, never changed.

"Why not?" She glanced at the two boys. "It's fun to spoil kids."

"Maybe this isn't going to be so bad after all," Danny confided to Joey.

Caroline smiled, though she gave no indication of having heard. "Well, I need two big strong young men to help me with my groceries. Know where I can find some?"

"Me—I'm a big strong young man." Joey held up his hand.

"Are not." Danny sneered. He looked up at Caroline. "I am."

They raced each other to Caroline's car in the driveway.

Sloan shook his head, following in their wake to see what needed carrying. So much for hoping the boys would be on their best behavior. He glanced at Caroline over his shoulder.

"You asked for it," he reminded her.

"Yes," she murmured, unable to contain her grin as she followed them to her car, "I did."

Chapter 3

"Are you sure they're not in your way?"

Sloan looked dubiously at his sons. Danny and Joey were flanking Caroline, shadowing her every move, each trying to outdo the other. He wasn't sure just what had gotten into them. He couldn't remember them ever being quite this enthusiastic before. As for the kitchen, it was in a state of organized chaos, if there was such a thing.

Joey looked over his shoulder, his arms filled with the two boxes of lasagna noodles Caroline had asked him to get from the table. His grin nearly split his generous mouth.

"We're not in the way, Daddy. We're helpers." He held his head up proudly as he looked at Caroline for confirmation. "Right, Caroline?"

His smile might be Julie's, but the rest of him reminded her of a miniature Sloan. The boy was positively edible.

"Right." She took the boxes from him. Opening the

first, she gingerly began sliding the wide pieces of pasta into the boiling water, two at a time. Standing on a step stool next to her, Danny was solemnly stirring the sauce as if the fate of the free world depended on it.

Caroline had worked nothing short of magic, Sloan thought in admiration, the way she'd harnessed the boys' energy and turned it productive. Still, he felt Danny and Joey were being just a bit too familiar, calling her by her first name.

Bending down to Joey's level, he turned the boy around to face him. "Maybe you should call her Dr. Masters," Sloan suggested.

Joey's mouth drooped until it was a borderline pout. He slanted a look toward Caroline to see whether she agreed to this barrier being imposed on their friendship.

A heartbreaker, just like his dad. The thought assailed Caroline out of the blue. Shutting it away, she came to Joey's aid.

"And maybe you should see if you can scare up a pan large enough for this feast." Caroline fixed Sloan with a telling look. "It's the only thing I didn't think to bring."

Joey was still waiting.

She set his mind at ease. "I don't mind them calling me Caroline. I get enough of 'Dr. Masters' at the clinic." She looked around at her work crew. "We're all friends here, right?"

"Right," the boys chorused, pleased to be placed on equal footing with an adult.

Sloan knew when he was outnumbered. Moving Joey out of his way, he crouched down and opened the lower cupboard doors. A jumble of pots that never managed to remain neatly stacked greeted him. Of course, he thought, shoving some to the side as he began to rummage, he'd never gotten around to properly stacking them, either.

As a lid clattered to the floor, he glanced in Caroline's direction. She'd brought fresh ground beef, spices, two kinds of cheeses, and everything else that went into making a home-cooked meal. To the undiscerning eye, it looked like the beachhead of an invasion.

"You really don't have to go to all this trouble, you know."

He'd already said that. "I told you, cooking relaxes me." Taking the long-handled wooden spoon from Danny, she sampled the sauce. A little more mozzarella, she decided. Shredded flakes drizzled from her fingers as she tossed a handful in. "And right now," she murmured, almost to herself, "I could really use something to make me relax." Handing the spoon back to Danny, she began emptying the second box of pasta.

Something in her voice caught his attention. Sloan rose, placing two long pans on the counter. "Take your pick." He studied her face. "Life in the big city too hectic for a small-town girl like you?"

She hadn't meant to let that last comment slip. This wasn't the time or the place to go into what was bothering her.

"Last time I looked, Bedford wasn't such a small town. It's growing up real nice." She lapsed into a twang on purpose. It was an inside joke.

He caught it and laughed. She sounded exactly like an English teacher they'd once had. Mr. Cotton. Hearing the man read Shakespeare with a southern drawl had put an entire new spin on the plays.

"Some would say so have you." He'd no sooner said it than he saw color creep up her cheeks. Surprised, curious, Sloan couldn't help himself. He lightly grazed her cheek with the tips of his fingers. "Caroline, is that a blush?"

It was, and it was stupid, she told herself. Stupid to react to him like this, after all this time. He had meant nothing by the comment and probably wasn't even aware that he'd touched her.

Her cheek felt warm.

Caroline pretended to sniff. It amused the boys to see their father put in his place. "The kitchen's hot—for those of us who are moving around. Those of us who aren't helping are invited to sit on the sidelines and out of the way."

With that, she turned away from him. Only then did she discreetly drag air into her lungs, hoping to halt the wild flutter that had accompanied the damn burst of color to her cheeks. She was behaving just like a schoolgirl.

Just the way she had when she harbored her silent crush on him.

A lot of years had gone by since then, she reminded herself. She'd been over Sloan for a long time.

Raising his hands in surrender, Sloan backed off with a laugh and sat down at the kitchen table. He watched her work for a moment. Caroline certainly did know her way around a kitchen, he thought. And around kids. She seemed to know exactly what to say to Danny and Joey to get them to cooperate.

A man could learn something from a woman like that, he mused.

She could feel his eyes on her. Caroline had to harness her thoughts before they could flourish and take flight. More than likely, Sloan wasn't even aware he was looking at her. Caroline glanced over toward him. He *was* staring.

"What?"

"You didn't answer my question, you know," he reminded her.

She checked on the sauce. It was getting a tad too thick. "Now you sound like a teacher."

"I am a teacher."

She heard pride in his voice. "A good one?"

Hungry, Sloan picked up a handful of mozzarella from the dish where she'd placed it and nibbled. "The principal seems to think so."

Caroline was willing to bet that half the girls in Sloan's classes thought so, too. And had huge crushes on him. She would have if he was her teacher.

She shook her head in wonder. Life took funny turns. "Who would have ever thought that you would actually voluntarily return to the academic scene." Crossing to the table, she slapped his hand away from the mozzarella before he could take any more. "In high school, you were always dying to get out."

The boys exchanged looks and giggled. Caroline was treating their dad the same exact way she was treating them.

With a sigh, Sloan dropped his hand, and Caroline returned to her post by the stove. "I had things to do, people to be with."

There was a sadness in the reply, and she knew he was thinking about Julie, even though he'd deny it if she made the assumption out loud.

He shrugged. "Things look a little different on the other side of the desk." Getting up, he crossed to the hub of activity, joining Joey. He looked pointedly at Caroline. "You *still* didn't answer my question. Are things too hectic for you in Albuquerque?" Was she thinking of relocating? It would be nice to have her to talk to once in a while.

There was no harm in talking about that. "With a capital *H*," she admitted. "But it's a good hectic, and I love it. Hot and cold running kids, making a difference, it's just what I want."

Joey was trying very hard to follow the conversation. He liked listening to grown-ups talk and wanted very much to understand. He tugged on Caroline's sleeve, and she gave him her attention instantly. He liked that. "Why are the kids hot and cold and where are they running to?"

"Kids always run," she answered. "And it's just a joke."

He knew about jokes. Timmy Smith was always telling him jokes and riddles in school. This didn't sound like anything Timmy would have said. "Do I hafta be big to unnerstand?"

Caroline pretended to consider. "Maybe a little bigger than you are," she conceded.

He didn't mind that, as long as he wasn't alone. "Bigger than Danny." Joey nodded toward his brother. "'Cause he don't unnerstand, either."

Danny opened his mouth to retort. Caroline could see where this was going. An ounce of prevention was needed here.

"Danny, why don't you bring me that jar of tomato sauce over there?" She pointed toward it. "I think we might need a little extra."

Danny hopped off the stool, hoping Caroline was watching as he landed effortlessly on the balls of his feet. Like a cat, he thought. No, better than that. A panther. Quickly he fetched the jar.

"Thank you." She started to pry off the lid—except

it wouldn't give. Caroline gripped the lid more firmly and tried again. Nothing.

Sloan smiled to himself as he watched her struggle. She'd always been a little stubborn, he thought. He remembered the three of them studying math together. Caroline would always stick it out until she could find a solution to the problem, no matter how difficult it was. She never gave up. It was an admirable quality. Usually.

He put out his hand. "I just love a damsel in distress. It's the English teacher in me," he confessed. There was amusement in her eyes as she looked at him. "I think you might need a little muscle here."

"I got muscles," Danny declared, flexing his thin arm for Caroline and desperately trying to make a muscle appear.

She felt his biceps and nodded solemnly. "Very impressive, but I think your dad's are just a wee bit bigger. Goes with his size," she added, with a wink that assuaged Danny's disappointment.

Caroline surrendered the jar to Sloan. "I always knew you'd come in handy for something."

"How about the time I bailed you out of jail?" he reminded her wryly, opening the jar.

"You were in jail?" Danny cried. He didn't know whether it was all right to be impressed, but he secretly was.

"It was a protest against using animals in lab experiments, and I wasn't even protesting," she told the awestruck duo. "I was trying to talk your mother out of being there. Unfortunately, that was just the moment the police decided to come. Your mom managed to get away, but I didn't."

"And they put you in jail?" Joey's eyes were huge.

"Did you cry?" He knew he would if someone put him in jail, away from his dad and Danny.

"No." But she had felt like it at the time, Caroline recalled. It had been useless to protest that she had been arrested by mistake. That was everyone's story. "Your mom called your dad, and he bailed me out before my parents could find out." He'd come to her rescue, she thought fondly, just like a knight in shining armor. It hadn't mattered that he was someone else's knight; just the fact that he had come had always meant a lot to her.

Sloan made no comment. He shouldn't have said anything, however flippant. He didn't want to talk about anything that remotely had to do with the past and Julie. Leaning over the pot as Caroline stirred in the last of the tomato sauce, he took a deep breath. The aroma swirled around him, reminding his stomach that it was running on empty. "Smells good."

Joey puffed up his chest. "I already told her she did."

Caroline laughed, feeling just a shade embarrassed. "Your dad means the sauce." She began to take the noodles out of the pot one by one, lining them up on a plate to cool.

Joey wasn't ready to let the point go. "But she does, doesn't she, Dad?"

Sloan pretended to sniff Caroline's hair, for Joey's benefit. The very subtle perfume scent of roses blooming in the spring rose up above the aroma of the simmering sauce, filling his senses in an unexpected rush. Sloan looked at Caroline, surprised that something so sensual could be associated with her. He'd never thought of Caroline in those terms.

"Yes," he said slowly, "she does."

The playful look had melted away from Sloan's face. Something tightened in her stomach in response. Afraid that Sloan might notice the effect he was having on her, Caroline focused her attention on retrieving the last of the pasta from the pot. She dipped the slotted spoon in too far and yelped as her fingers skimmed the boiling water. The spoon clattered to the stovetop.

Jumping off the stool, Danny grabbed her by the arm and tugged her toward the sink. "Quick, put it under cold water. G-mama does it all the time," he added when she looked at him in surprise. He turned on the faucet for her.

Sloan was about to remind his son that Caroline *was* a doctor, but never got the chance.

Caroline did as she was told. "I think you have a budding doctor here," she told Sloan.

Danny flushed with pleasure. "Nah, I don't like all that blood and stuff."

"That's just a small part of it. Mostly it's about helping people, and you've got a nice touch." Caroline shut off the water. "Why don't you think about it?"

It was the first time anyone had treated him like a grown-up. Danny puffed up his chest. "Maybe I will," he said in his very best grown-up voice.

"Good." Caroline pulled the first pan over to her. "Okay, troops, we're going to handle this as if it were an assembly line."

"What's a 'sembly line?" Joey asked.

"That's when everyone has a different, but equally important, job." Caroline congratulated herself on her diplomacy. "I'm going to put down the pasta layers, then you're going to spread the sauce," she explained, looking at Danny, "and you're going to sprinkle the mozzarella," she told Joey.

"What's Dad going to do?" Danny wanted to know.

"The ricotta." Caroline pulled the large container out

of the refrigerator, where she'd placed it, and presented it to Sloan.

He turned the container around in his hand. "Think I can handle it?"

"Sure." She gave him a spoon. "As long as you don't spread it too thin."

Sloan took off the lid and set it on the counter. "I never spread things too thin."

That, Caroline thought, was a matter of opinion.

"Another helping?" Caroline held up the spatula and looked around the dining room table at the other three occupants for any takers.

Joey and Danny both moaned, holding their stomachs. "No, thank you," Danny murmured.

"We did good, huh?" Joey asked her as he held the elastic on his waistband away from his full tummy.

Her heart felt warm, the way only the company of a child could make it. "We did good."

Sloan looked at what remained in the pan. There was less than a quarter left. He'd had no idea he'd consumed so much. Right now, he really envied Joey the elastic on his pants. He shouldn't have had that third serving, but it had been a long time since he ate so well. His mother, bless her, couldn't hold a candle to Caroline.

He sighed. "The next sound you will hear is the three Walters men, exploding."

Joey giggled, adding to Sloan's feeling of contentment. That, too, had been missing for a very long time.

Caroline laid the spatula down. "So I guess ordering pizza is out of the question?" She looked directly at Danny.

Danny sank down farther into his seat as he shook his head.

"This was better than pizza," Joey said quickly. Never shy, he eagerly asked, "Can you come and do this again?"

"While I'm in town, sure." Caroline's eyes shifted toward Sloan. He hadn't said anything to second the motion. "As long as your dad doesn't mind."

"He doesn't mind," Danny put in quickly.

"Yeah," Joey chimed in. "He was smiling when he put the plates on the table."

"No secrets in this house," Sloan said with a shake of his head. But he didn't really mind—after all, this was just Caroline.

Automatically she reached for Joey's plate and placed it on top of hers. Efficiency was something she lived by, half from habit, half from necessity. Her eyes were still on Sloan.

"I take it you don't smile very often?"

He lifted a shoulder carelessly. "I forget from time to time." He slanted a silencing glance at his youngest, who was completely oblivious to it. "Amazing the amount of information you can manage to gather without pumping the informants."

Her smile filtered into her eyes. "I have a gift."

That she did, he realized. Sloan looked at her, intrigued. Caroline looked pretty—glowing, almost. Had she always looked like that? He couldn't remember.

Rousing himself, Sloan rose. Caroline, he'd noticed, hadn't eaten very much. Not like the rest of them. Something about a chef not eating his own food came back to him.

They both reached for the pan together, their fingers brushing. They always seemed to be coming from opposite directions, he thought, remembering the clang of the supermarket carts as they'd crashed into each other.

He held his end, even as she held on to hers. "No, you cooked, I'll clean up," he told her, tugging a little. "It's only fair."

She liked being busy, and Sloan looked as if he sorely needed a break from his routine. "I wasn't aware that this was a treaty."

He looked down at her hands expectantly, and Caroline finally withdrew them. "You've gotten a lot more assertive since we were in high school," he told her as he headed toward the kitchen.

"I've had to," she called after him.

He wanted to ask why, but decided that was none of his business. She'd tell him if she wanted to. Besides, he really didn't want to talk about anything serious tonight. Caroline had ushered in a relaxed air with her, and he wanted to hang on to it for as long as he could.

Depositing the pan in the back of the refrigerator, he took out something he'd been saving. He grinned to himself as he opened the box he'd picked up from the bakery on the way home tonight.

"You still have a weakness for chocolate?" he asked, raising his voice.

She laughed in response, giving him his answer. "Does the sun still rise in the east in the morning?"

"I don't know. Does it?" He came out carrying a chocolate cream pie before him. The whipped cream on top was almost perfect. Appreciative squeals came from his sons, but his eyes were on Caroline. "Lately I've been too busy to notice."

Caroline let out a long, sensual sigh as he set the pie down in front of her. "That looks positively decadent."

Sloan retreated to get plates and forks. "We could just look at it all evening."

Getting to her feet, she took the plates from him and

distributed them, moving the ones they'd used at dinner to one side. "*You* could look at it all evening—me, I plan to do something more satisfying than just looking."

"Can we have a piece, Dad?" Danny asked eagerly.

Sloan raised an eyebrow. Danny had eaten more than any of them. "I thought you were stuffed."

Caroline understood. "Not where chocolate cream pie's concerned. There's always room for chocolate cream pie, right, boys?"

They beamed at her, their full stomachs a thing of the past. "Right," they chorused.

Picking up the knife, Caroline took over. She cut a wide wedge of pie for each boy, and then one for Sloan. This time, he noted, the piece she took for herself was just as large as theirs.

Nice to know that some things didn't change, he mused. And then he stopped, fascinated, as he watched her take her first bite. Caroline's eyes fluttered closed. A look that couldn't be called anything but sensual took over her face.

"You look like you're in ecstasy."

Her eyes opened, and a hint of a flush brushed against her cheeks again, but she smiled. "I am. I love chocolate."

He found himself wondering why a woman like Caroline wasn't married yet. Some man deserved to see that expression on her face when it didn't involve chocolate.

"You're not eating, Daddy. Want me to help you?" Joey volunteered, his fork ready to commandeer the slice.

"You stick to your own, sport. I'll handle this." He was aware of Caroline's laughter as he began to eat. It was a nice sound.

The evening flew by. All too soon, it was over and

he was walking her to her car. Sloan resisted the temptation to linger, to hang on to the peaceful feeling for just a little longer. Selfishly he hoped her stay in Bedford wouldn't be a short one. For the first time in a long time, that haunted feeling that always seemed to find him in the evening hadn't come.

He placed the huge pot she'd brought with her on the passenger side and closed the door, then turned to face Caroline. "Thanks."

The word, pregnant and solitary, hung in the air, unadorned. "For what?"

Sloan shrugged as he leaned against her car. Where did he begin?

"For dinner. For getting along so well with the boys." His eyes swept over Caroline. God, it was good to see her again. To feel normal again, for a little while. "For your company. Take your pick."

Everything had changed, and nothing had changed. She still wanted there to be more in his look than there was. She knew he saw her only as a friend, and she cherished their friendship, but still, there was a tiny part, a very tiny part, that rebelled. That wanted.

That was it, she thought—it wanted and it couldn't have.

Annoyed with herself, she widened her smile for Sloan's benefit. "I'll take all of the above, and you're welcome. But it was you who came to my rescue."

Several times during the evening, he'd gotten the feeling that something was on her mind, something she wasn't ready to talk about. Maybe she wanted him to prod. "How's that?"

"I needed to get away tonight." She sighed, guilt nibbling at her for feeling this way. "It was nice to find refuge with an old friend."

His eyes searched her face. "What's bothering you, Caroline?"

She shrugged, looking away. She wasn't going to burden him with her problems. He had enough of his own. Besides, this was family business. "Maybe I am a little overworked. My batteries need a little recharging."

It wasn't that, he thought. "If that's the way you act on low voltage, I'd hate to be in your path when you're fully charged. I don't remember your being quite this energized, and I'm too young to have my memory begin failing just yet." He saw something flicker in her eyes. Pain? Why? What had he said?

The smile was forced, blanketing her feelings, meant to smother any questions he might have. "I'm a late bloomer. Maybe it's because my work is so demanding." She rounded the hood to the driver's side. "Or maybe I just realized that life goes by too fast, and you can't miss a minute of it, so you've got to grab all you can."

Her remark hit too close to home. "It's never enough," he told her quietly, blocking the ache that threatened to come. "No matter how much you grab, it's never enough."

He and Julie had been together since they were both fifteen. That had given them sixteen years. Sixteen years of being boyfriend and girlfriend, lovers, fiancé and fiancée and finally husband and wife. But those sixteen years were all in the past, and he was standing in the present. Without her.

Caroline placed a hand on his shoulder, wanting to comfort him, not knowing how any more now than she had when Julia died. All she could do was point to the positive and hope it would help.

"I know. But you're doing well. The kids look happy and healthy. And well cared for."

He blew out a breath. The kids. It felt as if he were always shortchanging them. "I don't spend nearly enough time with them. School keeps me busier than I thought it would."

"They don't seem to be suffering." She grinned, thinking about Danny and Joey, the way they'd fought each other to help her. "I'm crazy about them."

The kind of pride he'd never known existed until Danny was born spread out through his chest. "It seems to be mutual. Even Danny came around, and he's usually the tough one. Joey would sell his heart to any pretty lady who came along."

Pretty. The word sprang out at her. He'd called her pretty. Caroline knew he'd said it without thought, but it warmed her all the same.

Their eyes met and held. He saw compassion in hers. But then, Caroline had always been sympathetic, and so easy to talk to. He'd missed her, he realized. A lot. "I appreciate you coming over."

"I appreciate being asked over," she said in the same tone, then laughed.

He opened the car door for her, and then paused. "Maybe we can do this again before you leave. How long are you staying?"

She had put in for a month, but maybe that wasn't enough. Or maybe, when the tests were done and she'd spoken to the specialists, she'd discover that her fears were groundless. If that was the case, she'd be back at the clinic sooner than that. "I'm not sure. That all depends on circumstances."

His mouth curved. "You're being very mysterious."

"Not mysterious, just..." She let her voice trail off.

Something *was* wrong, he thought. Really wrong. He'd been too caught up in his own world to realize that. Sloan took her hand and drew her away from the car. "Want to talk?"

She did, but what was there to say? It would be best if there was something concrete to go on before she voiced her concerns to anyone. There was no use in jumping to conclusions, although right now, it didn't seem like a jump so much as a small step.

"No, it's late and it's a school night." The phrase, one she'd heard so often from her parents, made her want to laugh. It felt good to tease him. "We'd better call it a night."

"Yeah, you're right. Thanks again for coming." He leaned over to kiss her cheek.

Caroline threw her purse in next to the pot. She turned her head to say it was her pleasure. And that was when it happened. Her lips brushed against his. The contact was so brief that for a second she thought she only imagined it happening. Imagined it the way she had so many times before, when she was younger.

The jolt that went through her told her it was real.

Her heart held its breath, then began to beat wildly, like a frantic camper trying to beat out a flame that had leaped out of the campfire and threatened to burn through the brush.

The overwhelming desire to kiss her, really kiss Caroline, came to him without warning, so intense that it sucked his breath away. He almost gave in, and then control took hold.

But his body still tingled.

What the hell was that all about? he thought.

Belatedly he remembered to breathe. His lungs were aching, as if they were going to burst. Sloan let the breath out slowly, then dragged his hand through his hair. He smiled at her sheepishly.

"Sorry."

Sorry. He was sorry, she thought. He'd kissed her, and it had been a mistake.

Of course it had been a mistake. Sloan would never...

Rousing herself, Caroline shook her head at his apology. "Friends never have to say they're sorry, Sloan."

She got into the car quickly, and drove away before he could say anything else.

Chapter 4

The sight of her father sitting on the front porch swing when she pulled up in the driveway drew Caroline out of her mental fog. This was why she was here, why she'd returned to Bedford, to take care of her family. Not to try to somehow kindle dampened fires that wouldn't burn.

"Hi, Dad."

Joshua smiled as she walked up the two steps to the house. He patted the seat next to him in a silent invitation. "How did dinner go?"

She dropped down on the swing beside him. "Fine." The answer came out too quickly, and she knew it. So did her father, to judge by the look on his face. She didn't want to talk about Sloan just yet, not after what had just happened. Not until all the feelings were ironed out and tucked neatly away. She knew the danger in making something out of nothing. "What are you doing out here?"

Joshua nodded toward the sky. "Looking at the stars. It's a beautiful night," he murmured in awed appreciation. He gazed at them as if he'd never really seen stars before. "Ever notice how small they make you feel? The stars," he clarified. His mind had been hopscotching around so much this last hour or so, he wanted to be sure he made his thoughts clear when he spoke. "They're supposed to be so big, and yet, they're just pinpricks in the sky." He looked at his daughter. "What does that make us?"

An emotion she couldn't quite read was in his eyes. Fear? Confusion? She didn't know.

"People," she answered simply. "With lives and goals and responsibilities to those we love."

Joshua stopped rocking and focused on his daughter's face. "I know you too well, Carrie. What are you getting at?"

He knew the answer to that, too, she thought. He was too intelligent not to. Maybe he was just hoping she'd say something else. She began at the most logical place. "Mother's worried about you."

He laughed softly. "Your mother wouldn't be happy if she didn't have something to worry about."

"Fuss about, not worry," Caroline corrected. Guilt and defiance passed over his face. She let neither put her off. "You've got to see a doctor, Dad."

Not saying anything, he shut his eyes. After a moment, she placed her hand on his arm, fear rippling through her like the rings formed by a rock tossed into a stream. "Dad? What's wrong?"

He opened his eyes reluctantly and looked at her. Belatedly, a tired smile followed. "Nothing. I'm just trying to absorb the moment. To seal it in, and maybe manage to keep it somehow. It's been a long time since we just sat here like this, talking. Too long. I want to remember everything." He sighed, restless, edgy. "I want to remember."

She understood. In his own way, he'd just admitted that he knew something was wrong with him. She felt so helpless. "How bad is it?"

Joshua shrugged. "Not bad, really. I forget things sometimes." As soon as the words were out, he wished he hadn't said them. "Just a few things here and there, that's all. A man my age is bound to forget some things. There are a lot of thoughts rattling around in this old head."

He wasn't fooling her. Or himself. Caroline's heart ached for him. "It's more than that, isn't it, Daddy? More than just the occasional thing."

Sadness gave way a little to pleasure. "You haven't called me Daddy in a long time."

She began to protest, but then realized that he was right. When was the last time she'd called him that? When was the last time she'd sat down and had a lengthy conversation with this man she'd all but idolized as a child? She couldn't really remember. It didn't change how she felt about him.

"But you are. You've always been Daddy to me." Her very lovable, very stubborn daddy. "I don't want to lose you," she said fiercely.

That made two of them. "I don't want to be lost."

Caroline squeezed his hand, as if she could squeeze out his cooperation. "Then agree to see a doctor. At least Dr. Wiseman."

Joshua rose. With his back to his daughter, he leaned against the railing that ran the length of the porch and looked up at the sky again, seeing only the darkness this time.

His voice drifted back to Caroline. "If I do, I might have to face something I don't want to."

She crossed to him. The set of his shoulders looked so sad, she thought. Sagging. As if he were already accepting defeat. This wasn't the man she knew.

"I think you already are," Caroline said gently.

But he shook his head. "No, I'm facing the possibility of something. There's a world of difference between that and knowing."

"Daddy, please." With understated urgency, Caroline took his hand in hers, forcing him to look at her again. She pleaded with him. "You've always helped me. For once, let me help you."

He said nothing for a long time, but then finally nodded. "All right. Make the appointment with the old quack. I'll go." Some of his former spirit returned to his eyes. "But I won't like it."

"You don't have to like it, just go." She didn't want to think about the future, about what might be. She just wanted to remember him this way, here with her, talking. "Thanks, Daddy."

"Thanks, nothing. You owe me, and don't you forget it."

His choice of words, Caroline thought, was ironic without being meant to be.

Dr. Benjamin Wiseman spent a long time shut away in the examination room with her father. So long that Caroline began to get fidgety, not knowing whether it was a good sign or not. Wiseman was only a general practitioner, but that allowed a wide spectrum of medicine to touch his life, and he'd been a doctor for thirty years. That translated into a vast amount of acquired knowledge and information. Caroline hoped that meant he'd somehow have the answer to questions she didn't really want to ask.

Leaving his patient to get dressed, Wiseman stepped out of the examination room and motioned for Caroline to follow him to his office.

"I'm surprised your mother didn't come along," he began abruptly.

There was no question in her mind that he knew her parents better than she did. They were not only doctor and patients, they socialized outside the office. "I think she was afraid to. She doesn't take bad news well. The longer she can put it off, the better."

Wiseman nodded as he sat down. "Your father's always sheltered her. Not a great many women like that left."

Caroline merely nodded. She wasn't here to talk about her mother. Caroline took one of the two chairs before his wide, cluttered oak desk. She could remember a time when she had felt dwarfed by its size. She waited as he wrote something in her father's file. Then, sitting on the edge of the chair, she asked the question that had ridden shotgun with her ever since her mother's phone call broke into her sleep.

"Do you think it's Alzheimer's disease?"

Wiseman closed the manila folder and peered at her over the tops of his half glasses. "I don't know," he said honestly. He'd listened to what Caroline had to say when she called him prior to her father's appointment. And, more important, he had listened to his patient. His verdict was undecided. "There's no test for Alzheimer's," he reminded her.

She knotted her hands in her lap. It looked as if she were praying, she realized suddenly. Maybe, in a way, she was.

"I know, but he might have something else." *Oh, please, let him have something else.* "The symptoms he's been exhibiting can be attributed to a number of other causes. That's why I want you to authorize tests for him. Everything you can think of. I want all the possibilities ruled out. Hypothyroidism, lesions, a toxic reaction to drugs," she said. "Everything. I don't want my father being told he has Alzheimer's unless we're absolutely sure it's nothing else."

Wiseman envied Joshua the love he saw in Caroline's eyes. He had no children of his own to worry about him. "Do you want me to recommend a specialist?"

"He won't go to a specialist. I could hardly get him to agree to come to you. For now, why don't you handle his case? He trusts you. And so do I." She saw the small, faraway smile that rose to the doctor's lips. "What?"

"I was just remembering you as a little girl, your heels all but dug into the carpet as you refused to come into my office. Your mother and my nurse had to practically carry you in so you could get your shots for school. And now look at you, a doctor yourself."

She vividly remembered the fear she had experienced that day. Remembered, too, just how kind the doctor had been to her. He'd taken the time to talk to a frightened young girl, instead of rushing off to his next patient. She'd grown up wanting to be that kind of doctor. "I had a great example to go on."

His eyes twinkled. "Good. Nice to know I'm appreciated." Leaning forward, he studied her face. "Have you given any thought to coming back to Bedford to practice?"

Well, that was out of the blue. Caroline shrugged. She supposed it had been in the back of her mind in one form or another since she got her degree. "I've taken a temporary leave of absence from the clinic. To be honest, right now, I don't know what my plans are."

"Dr. Brady is thinking of retiring. His practice is up for sale." Wiseman steepled his fingers before him thoughtfully. "At least come and work at the hospital. Temporarily, of course," he added quickly, before she could turn him down. "We've always got a slot opened in the ER, and you've got a very levelheaded, soothing manner about you. You'd be just what the doctor ordered, so to speak." He chuckled at his own comment.

She saw through his words. "Why this interest in keeping me busy?"

He wasn't going to insult her by making up excuses. "You know as well as I do that a disease doesn't just hit the person, it hits that person's family, as well. You need something to keep you from climbing the walls while you wait this out, and we need another doctor. Hal Endicott just left. Something about moving to Arizona or New Mexico, one of those desert states." He himself was a native Californian, and had never experienced a desire to be anything else. "I've got some pull with the board. I can push the paperwork through. You could be on staff by tomorrow. Besides," he said as a grin split his face, "I wouldn't want you to get rusty. Harris Memorial could always use a fine young pediatrician."

He was taking a great deal on faith, she thought. "How would you know whether or not I'm a fine pediatrician? I might be a very mediocre doctor."

"Not you." She could tell he meant that sincerely. "I told you, I have connections. Besides, your mother never missed a chance to tell me about how you were doing in school. Every visit, there she was, whipping out grades, or newspaper clippings about her daughter the doctor." He looked at Caroline, making his pitch in earnest. "So how about it? You're going to be here for a while, anyway. Your parents need you. And we could use the extra pair of hands."

She thought about it for a moment. It might be a good solution at that. She was already feeling antsy, and she'd been here only a few days. How would she feel after a week or two? Maybe the doctor was right. "All right, start pushing paperwork. I don't like standing around, being useless."

Dr. Wiseman laughed off the thought. "You, Caroline, could never be useless. It's not in your makeup." He shook her hand, well pleased. "You won't regret this. And who knows? Maybe you'll like it well enough at Harris to stay."

"I'm always open to possibilities," she said to him. "And the tests for my father?" Caroline asked, getting back to the reason they were in his office in the first place.

Wiseman began to write down a list of tests he wanted performed on his patient. "You get your dad down to the hospital and I'll do the rest." Tearing it off his pad, he handed her the authorization, then rose. "Now I've got to go in and talk to him, before he thinks we're plotting some sort of conspiracy against him."

Caroline joined him. "He'll think that anyway."

Wiseman laughed. "You certainly do know your dad, don't you?" His hand on her back, he escorted her out of the room.

Sloan rubbed his temples gingerly. The headache was getting to him. Both the internal one and the external one. The former came from tension; the latter was being caused by his students.

His eyes slightly squinted, he looked around at the

teenagers of all sizes and shapes who were scattered on the stage and in the first few rows of the auditorium. It was hard to believe that, somehow, he was expected to make a whole out of these various disjointed pieces.

The play just wasn't coming together.

It wasn't the only thing. He felt as if he were coming unglued himself. No wonder Mrs. Jacobs had gotten pregnant. He would have gotten pregnant, too, if it meant getting out of doing this play. Right now, it seemed as if everything that could go wrong was going wrong. Two of his leading characters and three of the lesser ones hadn't shown up for tonight's rehearsal. At least the leads had sent in excuses. The others hadn't even bothered.

He hated being tested like this. To add to his problems, he'd had to bring Danny and Joey with him to the rehearsal. Normally, he didn't mind. He could leave them in the care of one of the students and go on with his work. But, for some reason, the boys were really wired tonight. They were both acting up, and they just wouldn't listen when he told them to stop. Sloan could feel his temper being rubbed raw.

How could he expect to control his students if he couldn't even control his own kids?

"Headache, Mr. Walters?"

He nearly jumped as Allison came up behind him. It didn't help his head.

"Yes," he muttered, turning to the next scene in the script. Maybe this one would go better.

"I've got some aspirin," she offered. "I can just get—"

It wouldn't do any good. "This headache's beyond aspirin," he assured her. It was the kind of headache that wouldn't go away until he woke up in the morning.

Allison remained undaunted. "Maybe if I massaged it for you. I'm really very good."

He pulled his head away before she could place her fingers on his temples. "Thanks, but I think you'd better go and hit your mark."

Deflated, Allison did as he asked. Sloan looked at the students milling around behind him. "Okay, people, I know we're all tired here and this isn't Broadway, but you are going to be performing in front of your friends and family, and you don't want to embarrass them—or yourselves."

"Or you," Allison put in sweetly.

"I'm at the end of the food chain here, Allison," he said shortly. "But I want you to do yourselves proud. Now, I know you all have it in you. I was there at all the auditions, and I wouldn't have cast you in the parts if you didn't."

"Dad! Hey, Dad, look at me!" Joey called out behind him.

"Not now, Joey." What had gotten into the kids tonight? They were usually so good about coming here. "I'm busy."

"You're always busy," Joey said, pouting. "Just look at me! I'm an Indian, too!" he sang out in his squeaky, high-pitched voice.

Exasperated, Sloan turned around. He was going to have to find another baby-sitter, he thought. His mother's schedule was just too unpredictable these days. He couldn't fault her for it, just as he really couldn't fault the boys for being restless. He couldn't expect them to behave like still life paintings. They were too full of energy for that.

Sloan's throat constricted. Joey, intent on getting his attention, if just for a moment, was dancing along the edge of the stage, imitating the war dance that the Indians in Buffalo Bill's Wild West Show performed in the middle of the play. Just as Sloan opened his mouth to shout a warning, Joey's foot slipped, and he pitched, headfirst, off the stage.

Sloan rushed to catch him. He was too late. His hands caught fistfuls of air. Joey hit the floor, landing at his feet, his terrified shriek filling the room.

Everyone converged around them, wanting to help, not knowing how.

"Daddy?" Danny cried out fearfully, staring at his brother on the floor. There was blood on Joey's lower lip, and it was swelling fast.

"Someone call 911," Sloan ordered. He was only vaguely aware of movement behind him as someone ran out to summon an ambulance.

Fear clutched at his heart as Sloan dropped to his knees beside his son. Joey's eyes were open but dazed. He wanted to drag his small body to him, to gather him in his arms, but he knew the boy couldn't be moved.

Damn it, how could he have let this happen? "Joey, can you hear me?"

Joey's lips moved without making a sound. Sloan leaned over him, bringing his ear to Joey's mouth.

"I hurt, Daddy. Make it stop. Please make it stop."

"So, how was your first day?" Dr. Brian Herne, heretofore Harris Memorial's newest addition to the staff and fresh with a degree in orthopedics, gave Caroline what he thought was his best bedside smile. The one he *didn't* use on his patients. He'd shown Caroline the ropes when she had arrived for her shift today. That, he figured, entitled him to some quality time with her after hours. What kind of quality depended on her.

Caroline felt exhausted. The day had begun with an argument. Her father had changed his mind and staunchly refused to go in for the tests that had been ordered. She had all but threatened him with bodily harm if he didn't get into the car. She'd had to order her mother to come along, as well. Wanda had wanted to remain at home, safe in familiar surroundings. Hospitals frightened her. Caroline had marshaled both parents to the appropriate departments and remained with them the entire time.

Now there was nothing to do but wait for the results. She was grateful to Wiseman for suggesting that she take a position on the staff. It had certainly kept her mind, as well as her hands, occupied for the past few hours. There hadn't been time to take a break. Patients had been steadily rolling in until the past half hour, when the pace finally slacked off. She'd seen a potpourri of cases, varying from an accidental ear piercing with a fishhook to food poisoning to a really bad case of the flu. Then there had been the two campers covered with poison oak, blankets, and nothing else.

She was glad to see the day over, and she'd be even more glad to see the inside of her old room again and the bed that was in it.

This was not unlike her intern days.

She smiled at Herne. "I can see why Dr. Wiseman is so intent on roping people to come to work here. Is it always this crazy?" She shrugged the lab coat she'd been issued off her shoulders.

Herne helped her off with it. "This was one of the lighter days," he assured her. "Usually it's even crazier, although we have had more than our share of kids today." His eyes washed over her slowly, and he liked what he saw. A lot. "Where did you get your degree?"

"UCLA, then I interned at Scripps. I work at a clinic in Albuquerque now."

He gave her back the coat. "Albuquerque?" he echoed. "What are you doing here at Harris?"

Caroline tried to remember the way to the lockers. "That's a long story."

"I've got time. I'm off duty." His smile widened. "Want to grab a cup of coffee and tell me your long story?"

She shook her head. She had a feeling that he might be in the mood for something more than just talk. She'd come across more than one of his kind during her years of medical school and interning. Charming and godlike, he was the type who was eager to play doctor after hours.

"Not tonight, thanks. I'm tired, and…" her voice trailed off as the electronic doors in the rear of the ER flew open. Two paramedics hurried in, pushing a gurney between them. A small body lay in the middle of it.

Her heart stopped when she saw Sloan and Danny. She wasn't even aware of breaking into a run as she rushed toward them.

"Hey, you don't have to do that. You're off duty," Herne called after her.

"I just got back on." The words flew over her shoulder as she reached the gurney. Her eyes quickly washed over Danny, then Sloan, coming to rest on Joey. His face was bloodied. "Sloan, what happened?"

He had no idea what she was doing here, or who had called her; he only knew that he felt better because she was here. "Joey fell off the stage."

She looked at the paramedic. "I'm the attending physician here. What are his vital signs?" He rattled them off to her in the manner of a man who had been at his job a long time. Joey was stable and conscious, but whimpering like a puppy that had been badly abused. One hand was obviously hurt.

He clutched at her with his other one. "Am I gonna die?" Fear radiated from him.

"You're not going to die, Joey." Sloan's voice was gruff, choked by emotion he was trying to keep from surfacing.

But Joey needed more reassurance. "They took Mama to a hospital and she died."

Caroline placed her hand on his shoulder. "No, Joey, you're not going to die. I promise. I'm going to take care of you." She looked at the paramedics, signaling for a nurse to come help her. "Thanks, we'll take it from here."

"Can I stay with him?" Sloan asked.

She wouldn't have it any other way. "I think that might be for the best. He's a little scared."

Sloan blew out a breath. "He's not the only one."

Caroline indicated the empty area near the exit. It had just recently been vacated. There were two chairs positioned against a curtain that functioned as the only preserver of privacy.

"Make yourselves at home. This is going to take a while." She looked down at Joey. "This boy is going to X-ray."

"Are you going to come with me?" Joey asked.

"I have to. I'm the driver." She moved the gurney into position and began to push it toward the corridor herself.

The woman from the admissions desk blocked her way. She held up a clipboard with several papers attached to it. "You can't take him anywhere yet. The forms haven't been filled out."

Caroline nodded toward Sloan. "Mr. Walters will be happy to fill out any forms you want. He's a teacher, he's used to paperwork." Belatedly she remembered she still had her purse with her. Slipping the strap off her shoulder, she tossed it to Sloan. "Here, hold this for me. We'll be back as soon as we can." She draped her lab coat over the gurney.

The look of concern was still etched into Sloan's face. "It's going to be all right," she promised. "Trust me."

His eyes followed her out. "I do."

She knew he meant it.

It felt as if he'd been waiting forever. Danny was propped up against him, his head nodding to one side as the boy fought off sleep. It was a losing battle.

Sloan was too tense to sleep. He was too busy berating himself for not paying closer attention to his sons. They were what mattered, not some play that would be all but forgotten a week after it was performed.

By the time Caroline returned, walking beside Joey as an orderly pushed the gurney into the space beside the chairs, Sloan was ready to go looking for them.

He jumped to his feet, one hand holding on to Danny to keep his face from making sudden contact with the chair. Sloan saw the cast on Joey's arm. Was that the worst of it, or was there more?

Braced, he looked at Caroline. "So?"

"So, he's going to be just fine." She feathered her fingers through Joey's wheat-colored hair. It occurred to her that Sloan could do with some soothing himself.

"What about the cast? Is his arm broken?"

Caroline shook her head. "Not his arm, just his wrist. He broke it when he flung it out to break his fall. That'll heal before you know it. Quicker than if you had broken yours," she assured him. "Children are very resilient." She smiled at Joey. "Smart thinking, stopping your fall like that."

Joey wanted to take the credit, but his dad was here, and his dad had always said not to lie. "I was scared." He wondered whether she'd think less of him if he admitted that. She didn't look as if she did. Joey decided that Caroline was one pretty terrific lady, even if she was a doctor.

"I know you were, honey. You had every reason to be. Only cartoon heroes and stuntmen aren't afraid of falling off a stage." That seemed to reassure him of his manhood, Caroline thought, amused.

"And the bump on his head?" Sloan asked, prodding her.

Her eyes turned to him. "Is just a bump on the head. No concussion." She smiled. "His eyes are beautifully normal. Nothing else bruised or damaged, besides his split lip, and that didn't even need stitches, just some ice." She peered at Sloan's face. He did look a little worn around the edges. "How about you, how are you holding up?"

"Better," he admitted, "thanks to you." His eyebrows drew together, very much the way Joey's did, except that his were lighter and fuller. The color of wheat at sunset. Though marred by confusion, they were still sexy, she thought. The man was hopelessly sexy, even in a crisis.

Sloan couldn't recall Caroline mentioning working at the hospital the other night. And he'd realized into the first hour that no one had called her and told her about the accident. That had just been an absurd assumption on his part, brought about by his disjointed thoughts. He had to ask. "What are you doing here, anyway?"

Caroline thought of saying something flippant about coming to his rescue, but let it go. She kept it simple. "I got restless doing nothing. So I took a temporary position in the ER. Today was my first day." She looked at him more closely. "You look a lot worse than Joey does. Can I get you something?"

He shook his head. "I'm okay." Guilt and the taste of panic were already receding. It was just taking his heart a little while to catch up. "How long before I can take him home?"

Caroline considered the options. "Well, we could keep him here overnight for observation." She saw the frightened look entering Joey's eyes again. "Or you could take him home and keep an eye on him yourself."

Danny, standing silent throughout the discussion, moved closer to his brother. "I'll watch him," he volunteered solemnly.

Unable to resist, she cupped Danny's chin in her hand. "I know you will. Scared you, too, huh?"

Now that it was all over and Joey was getting all this attention, Danny saw no reason to confess that he had been afraid for his brother. "Nah, Joey's got a hard head. I knew he'd be okay."

Caroline nodded, pretending to be taken in. "Good thing your dad had someone levelheaded like you around. That's important to a future doctor, you know, having a level head." She watched, amused, as Danny's face lit up at her praise.

Sloan couldn't wait to get out of there. He'd never liked hospitals. They made him feel helpless, and he hated the feeling. He looked around. "Where's a phone around here?"

Caroline pointed to the lobby. "Through those doors. Why?"

"I need a taxi. We rode to the hospital in the ambulance. My car's still in the school parking lot."

"No problem." She picked up her purse from the floor, where Sloan had left it. "I'm off for the night. I can take you to your car and drive the boys home."

There was only so far he could impose. "You've already done enough."

Caroline wondered whether he was afraid that she expected something from him, after the other evening. Didn't he know her better than that?

"Hey, no extra charge," she said flippantly. "Unless... Any chocolate cream pie left?"

He couldn't remember. "If not, I'll have some delivered," Sloan promised.

"You can have my chocolate bar," Joey offered, wanting her to come home with him.

"Can't ask for more than that," she said warmly. Standing over him, Caroline extended her hand, waiting for Joey to shake it. "It's a deal."

Chapter 5

Dropping Sloan off in the high school parking lot, Caroline waited until he got into his car. Instead of transferring the boys, she just drove off with them, heading for their house.

She glanced up at the rearview mirror just as the light began turning yellow. Sloan was right behind her. She could have easily made it through, but he couldn't, and they would have been separated.

Caroline eased down on the brake.

She could barely make him out in her mirror. It was still enough to make her blood hum. There was no use telling herself any more stories. Nothing had changed for her. If anything, after being banked down for so long, the feelings she had for Sloan had just gotten stronger.

You'd have thought, after all these years, that she would have moved on.

She could have moved on all she wanted to, Caroline thought dryly, but it wouldn't have mattered. Wherever she went, she would have to take her heart with her, and her heart would always belong to Sloan. She might as well accept it.

Moving her foot onto the accelerator, Caroline turned toward the left. A Mercedes, switching lanes, cut in between them. Sloan's car faded to the rear.

Joey began to moan.

"We're almost there, Joey," she said, soothingly. "Just hang on a little while longer."

Caroline quickly angled the rearview mirror so that she could see into the back seat. Joey looked miserably uncomfortable. Poor little guy. She knew firsthand how tough it was to have a limb immobilized at that age. With her, it had been her leg. She'd tripped over the dog and gone tumbling down the stairs. A fractured tibia had been the result.

"It still hurts, Caroline." She could see that Joey was doing his best not to cry, but his lower lip was quivering. Caroline flipped the mirror back into place.

Entering Sloan's driveway, Caroline pulled up the hand brake and waited for Sloan to park beside her. She unbuckled her seat belt and turned around to look at Joey.

"It's going to hurt for a while, yet, honey. But you're being really brave about this." Leaning over, she squeezed his hand, lowering her voice as she shared a secret with him. "I know men twice your size who have acted like big babies when it came to pain."

His wrist was really hurting and throbbing within the cast, but it helped being called a man. Joey tried his best to look even braver.

"Really?"

"Really. Now, my advice to you is to sleep on your back tonight and put a pillow under your cast. If you keep it as still as possible, it won't hurt so much. And then, when you go back to school, you can get everyone to sign your cast. You'll be the hit of the first grade.'' In the distance, she saw Sloan's car approaching.

"Joey sleeps like a windup toy,'' Danny confided to her. "Kicking and turning all night. Dad found him on the floor last week. He was still sleeping.''

Julie used to sleep like that, she recalled, remembering sleep-overs they'd shared at each other's houses. Nothing short of a bomb could wake Julie up once she fell asleep.

Keeping a straight face, Caroline looked at Danny. "I guess then you're going to have to really watch him so he doesn't fall out. Big responsibility, Danny. Think you're up to it?''

He liked being treated like an adult. Caroline was quickly becoming one of his favorite people. "Sure.''

Sloan's car drew up beside hers. He shut off the engine and got out. "Ready to go in, Joey?''

Opening the rear door, Sloan stepped back to give Joey room. But it was Danny who got out first, and Danny who in turn took charge of his brother. Treating him far more gently than Sloan could remember, Danny placed a supporting hand around Joey's shoulders.

"You can lean on me if you want, Joey,'' he said solemnly.

Well, this was new. Sloan stood there, completely dumbfounded. Until this moment, Danny's relationship with Joey had been a typical one, based on sibling rivalry and one-upmanship.

Sloan glanced toward Caroline over the roof of the car. He had her to thank for this. He had her to thank for a lot of things, he thought. "This is a first.''

"He's growing up." She watched Danny lead Joey to the front door. "There's a very tender side to Danny."

Sloan could only shake his head in awe. "Not one that I've ever seen before." He rubbed the back of his neck, feeling the knots of tension there standing out like marbles. He was bushed. "Took you to bring it out."

Caroline shrugged. She wasn't very good at accepting compliments. "Just a matter of the right circumstances, nothing more." Time to go, she thought. She began to get into her car again. "Well, I guess I'll be seeing you."

Surprised, he rounded the hood, catching the door before she had a chance to close it. "Aren't you coming in?"

That was what she'd intended at the hospital, but on the ride home, she'd reconsidered. "So much has happened, I thought that maybe you'd want to be alone with your family right now."

He took her hand and drew her out of the car. "You *are* family, Caroline. I know it's not very manly to admit this, but I really don't know what I would have done if you hadn't been there tonight. God, Caroline, I'm not any good at this parenting thing."

That had been Julie's area of expertise, not his. He was good at earning a living, at being the strong silent partner, not at offering comfort to small boys with terror in their eyes. This was brand-new, uncharted territory he found himself in, and he would have killed for some kind of map showing him the way.

Caroline was that map, he thought. It came naturally to her, even without her having any children of her own. She had a talent for comfort.

She smiled at him. He was adorable when he was

helpless. "What are you talking about? You're doing just fine. All kids have accidents."

Maybe she would stay, she thought. Just for a little while. Since he wanted her to.

Caroline reached in the car for her purse and then slammed the car door shut. "You can't be everywhere at once."

Caroline meant well, but he couldn't hide behind excuses like that. Not when he was the only parent the boys had. He had to do better. "I feel like I should be."

"Well, don't," she said seriously. "That kind of thing is just going to make you crazy." *Physician, heal thyself,* she thought wryly. But it was hard to take her own advice. It was a lot easier just to give it. "Okay, I'll stick around for a while, get Joey settled in for the night."

It was stupid to feel so relieved because she was staying, but he did.

Gratitude underlined his smile, sending a salvo straight into her stomach and turning it upside down. "I'd appreciate it."

It was dumb of her to have even tried to fool herself into believing that she was ever going to be immune to him, Caroline thought as she followed Sloan up the brick steps that led to the front door. She might as well just accept her fate and be done with it. Part of her was always going to be a little bit in love with Sloan.

Or a lot.

When they reached the boys, Danny was pointing to the welcome mat. Four pink tea roses, wrapped in white tissue paper, lay across it. "Look, Dad, somebody left us some flowers. Maybe they're for you, Joey."

Joey eyed the roses. Flowers were for girls, not guys. "I'd rather have some ice cream."

"Tomorrow," Sloan promised. He knew for a fact

that there was nothing in the freezer but ice cubes. They'd eaten the last of the frozen dinners tonight, before going to rehearsal.

Sloan bent down to pick up the flowers. He had no idea who could have left them. Or why, for that matter. Joey was right—flowers were more of a girl thing.

There was a handwritten note attached to the paper with a pushpin. "'Hope he's feeling better,'" Sloan read. "'See you at rehearsal. I'll keep practicing for you. Allison.'"

Sloan looked so bewildered, staring at the roses, Caroline had to smile. "Looks like you have a groupie."

He wouldn't call Allison a groupie. She was just given to enthusiasm. Maybe a little too much enthusiasm. "My leading lady. The play's leading lady," Sloan corrected, annoyed at the slip.

He was still blind, wasn't he? she thought fondly. Just as blind now as he had been seventeen years ago. "I think you got it right the first time. This Allison of yours wants to be your leading lady."

He shoved the note into his pocket. The idea was absurd. "She's not mine, she's one of my students. And she's just a child."

If he believed that, he was even worse than she thought. With an eye on her impressionable audience, Caroline chose her words more carefully than she might have if they were alone.

"A kindergartner is a child, Sloan. Any female over the age of fifteen is a woman. Trust me."

"You weren't a woman at fifteen," he said. Sloan felt his other pocket for his house keys.

Yes, I was, you just never noticed. With a careless shrug, she let him go on believing what he wanted. "I was the exception. I was a bookworm. But Julie—Julie was a woman.''

His expression changed abruptly, freezing, as if he were trying to stave something off. He still wasn't prepared to go there, she thought. Until he was, he'd never be able to continue with his life.

Ignoring Caroline's comment and shoving the flowers under his arm, Sloan opened the door. Then he picked Joey up in his arms. ''Let's go, sport.''

The past few hours were beginning to take their toll. Joey fought to keep his eyes open. ''Where?''

Sloan headed for the stairs. ''To bed.''

He really wanted to go to bed, but if he did, he would miss all the fun. Joey struggled, trying to look wide awake. ''Can't I stay up and talk with you and Caroline?'' Twisting his head, he looked at his brother. ''Danny's staying up.''

Danny debated between doing the right thing and fighting for the right to remain up. It wasn't an easy decision.

Sloan made it for him. ''Danny's going to bed, too. It's late, we've all had a heck of a day, and you need your rest, buddy.''

Going up the stairs, Sloan led the procession to the boys' bedroom. It occurred to him that Danny wasn't protesting his decision. One small step for fatherhood, he thought.

Joey wasn't ready to give up. ''But I promised Caroline a chocolate bar.''

''I'll take a raincheck,'' Caroline said quickly.

Joey scrunched up his eyes, trying to understand. ''What's that?''

''That means you have to give it to me some other time.''

Joey's face lit up. "You'll come back?"

"I'll come back." Leaning over Sloan's arm, she brushed Joey's hair out of his eyes. "You're my patient, aren't you?"

A smile bloomed over his face. He didn't mind being a patient, as long as she was the doctor. Her hands had felt so nice and soft when she put the cast on him, it hardly hurt at all.

"Yeah."

"Okay, then, we have a deal. Now, how about Danny and I help you get ready for bed?" Without waiting for his reply, or for any comment from Sloan, she carefully scooped Joey out of Sloan's arms.

He liked it in Caroline's arms. He was closer to the nice smell. It reminded him a little of Mommy, he thought. She'd smelled good, too.

Joey looked at his dad. He looked really surprised, like he didn't think Caroline was going to carry him into the room. "What's Dad going to do?"

She looked at Sloan over her shoulder as she walked into the bedroom, Danny at her side. "He's going to get me that piece of chocolate cream pie he promised."

"Your wish is my command," Sloan said, turning on his heel.

If only that were true, she thought wistfully.

Fifteen minutes later, Caroline walked into the family room. She was alone.

Sloan was sitting on the sofa, waiting. There was a news broadcast playing on the television screen, but he had it on out of habit. He was too preoccupied to pay any attention to what was being said. Shifting in his seat, he looked behind her, but there was no shadow dogging Caroline's footsteps.

"Where's Danny?" Bedtime was always a difficult time. Neither Danny nor Joey ever wanted to go. Danny always had a hundred excuses for staying up. He'd figured that, despite his instructions to the contrary, Danny would come down with Caroline.

"Upstairs, in bed, guarding Joey." She had really enjoyed helping them get ready for bed. She'd even gotten in a short bedtime story. Danny had declared he was too old for "that kind of stuff," but she'd noticed that he listened just as intently as Joey when she read. "They're really very sweet together. I missed that kind of thing, being an only child."

As a parent, Sloan saw it from an entirely different perspective. "Yeah, but your parents had a lot more peace and quiet that way."

She thought of how sad they'd looked the day she left home for college. There'd been no one left at home to help fill the void. "That's one thing to call it."

"And another?"

That was easy. She perched on the arm of the sofa. "They missed out on twice the fun."

Fun. He had other names for it. "Things don't just double when you have a second kid, they explode. One and one never makes two, when it comes to kids," he told her wearily. "It makes an army."

Caroline leaned over, her eyes on his. Sloan wasn't fooling her for a second. "And you wouldn't trade them for anything in the world."

Sloan really didn't have to think about it, though he pretended to. "No, I wouldn't."

Caroline rose and picked up her purse. He'd assumed she was staying for a while. "Where are you going?"

She resisted the temptation to run her hand through his unruly hair, the way she had with Joey's. But her fingers still itched. "Home. I figure you've had enough stimulation for one day."

Her choice of words struck him. He hadn't thought of himself as being stimulated. Harried, half-crazed with worry, maybe, but stimulated? No. If he'd been stimulated at all, it had been the other night, when he stood with her by the car.

And kissed her.

Remembering brought the confusion he'd experienced back in vivid colors.

"Stimulated, huh? Is that what you call it now?" He laughed, but then his expression became more serious, as his eyes traveled over her face. Something nameless tugged inside him. "I think maybe I can stand a bit more. Why don't you stay for a little while? I'm out of pie, but I did find some hot chocolate."

For the first time, she noticed that there was a cup of hot chocolate sitting on the coffee table. He pushed it toward her. "Will that do?"

She arched an eyebrow, eyeing the cup. "Marshmallows?"

He looked toward the kitchen, thinking. The pantry left something to be desired, as far as orderliness went. It was the same with his life. "I don't think so. But I've got a half eaten box of raisins."

She shook her head. "I'll pass. But, what the heck, the chocolate's made, right? Can't let it go to waste."

Caroline sat down on the sofa, taking the cup in both hands. She felt her stomach tighten as her knees brushed against his, and told herself sternly that grown women with degrees in pediatric medicine weren't supposed to behave like this.

The first sip almost burned her tongue. "It is hot."

"Just made it." It hadn't been easy finding some.

He'd located what looked to be the last packet. "I thought I should be doing something with myself while you were saving my sanity."

She ventured another sip. This time, it didn't taste quite as hot. Her mouth was getting used to it. "Saving your sanity? You mean because I was getting them into bed?"

He nodded. "That's usually a time when they're at their worst."

They'd both been as docile as lambs with her. "I guess tonight's different."

Sloan was about to say something about the magical power she seemed to have over them, but he stopped. Maybe the magic wasn't restricted to his sons.

Or maybe he was just going crazy.

As much as he was resigned to it, he didn't like being a single father. Didn't like knowing that he'd forever be just a half, permanently separated from another half. Destined never to be whole again. At times, that made him lonelier than he thought he could possibly bear.

Yup, he was crazy.

He looked at Caroline. That same nameless thing was stirring within him. Getting larger. Just like the other night. But what? What was going on here, between them? What was it he felt? Was it just friendship? Stress? Or maybe something far more basic? Maybe his body was just rebelling against the celibacy that had been forced upon it.

But he didn't believe in sex for sex's sake. He never had.

None of it made sense to him. He really did feel like a man who was going slightly crazy.

"Yes," he finally agreed, sighing. "Tonight's different." He scrubbed his hands over his face. "I feel drained."

She was keeping him up, she thought, feeling guilty. "Then I should go."

She set the cup down, but he caught her hand, his fingers slipping around her wrist. What imprisoned her, though, was the look in his eyes. She couldn't read it, but she felt herself being drawn to it. Drawn into it. Drowning, just the way she had years ago. His eyes had always been such a dazzling shade of blue.

"No, don't leave yet. I want you to stay. Just for a little while longer." He knew he was being unreasonable, but he couldn't help himself. He needed her to stay, even if he couldn't put into words why. "Hell, Caro, you're the only thing that kept me together when I was at the hospital tonight."

She liked his being grateful to her, but she couldn't really take any credit. "I didn't spend much time with you," she pointed out.

She hadn't had to. "No, but you were there. And that made all the difference."

She could feel her heart beating faster, fueled by a hope that was absolutely baseless. There was nothing she could do about it. "Did it?"

"Sure. I knew that I had someone I could depend on. Someone I knew." He couldn't put it any better than that. Some English teacher he was. Sloan spread his hands helplessly. "I don't like hospitals."

She wondered whether he thought that was an admission of weakness. It wasn't such an unusual reaction. "Neither does my mother."

He barely heard her. In his mind's eye, he could see it all happening again. Could feel the horror, the fear, as he'd watched his son tumble down.

"When I saw Joey fall off the stage, his head aimed straight for the floor—"

Her hand covered his. "Don't go there, Sloan. He's okay. There's no reason to torture yourself with what-ifs." She knew that firsthand. Caroline looked at him, remembering afternoons she had spent alone with her daydreams. Daydreams that hadn't a prayer of coming true. "It never does any good."

"You're right." Absently he tucked a lock of hair behind her ear. "But I guess it's only human."

Her skin tingled where he had touched her. Couldn't he see what he was doing to her? Was he really that blind? No, she thought, he wasn't blind. He just saw her the way he had always seen her. As Julie's friend, and thus, by definition, his.

Somehow, she found her tongue. "Yes, it is."

Something in her voice made him look at her curiously. He regarded her in silence for a moment, questions flooding his mind. Questions mingling with half thoughts and warmed-over emotions.

"Why didn't you ever get married, Caroline?"

It was the last thing she'd expected him to ask. She tried to laugh off the question. "Now you sound like my mother."

"But why didn't you?" he asked, pressing her. It didn't make any sense to him, and he liked things to make sense. "You're great with kids, you've got a great sense of humor—"

She shuddered. She'd been there before. "And a terrific personality, yes, I know. That's the absolute kiss of death in a description for a woman." Caroline shook her head, wishing she could shake off the effects of his touch as easily. She could still feel his fingertips brushing along her face. "Like I said, you sound like my mother."

"Maybe that's because we both care about you." He had his share of friends, but none of them mattered to him as much as Caroline. None of them cared the way Caroline could care. "And you don't just have a great personality. You're pretty."

She tried not to let that get to her. "That's the second time you called me pretty. Keep saying it and I'm going to start believing it."

"You should. It's true." How could she look into the mirror every morning and not see that? Her features weren't exotic, as Julie's had been. They were more classic, subtle. Softly creeping up on a man when he least expected it. Infiltrating his thoughts until there was nothing else but her.

The thought caught him by surprise.

Caroline shrugged, uncomfortable. "To answer your question, I guess I've just been too busy, that's all." She looked away. "Maybe I just never met the right person."

With all the people she'd come into contact with in the past twelve years, he found that difficult to believe. "No one? In all this time?"

"There was someone," she said quietly, unable to help herself. "But he was already taken." Caroline got up. If she didn't leave now, she was going to say something she knew she'd regret in the morning. "Listen, the hot chocolate was terrific, but I think I should be going. You need your rest." She shifted, ready to beat a hasty retreat to the front door. She'd already said too much as it was. "I'm staying at my parents' house. You've got the number. If anything comes up with Joey during the night, don't hesitate to call. I'll be right over."

How typical. He rose beside her. "Caroline to the rescue."

Her knees felt uncomfortably shaky as she walked toward the door. That was what she got for venturing into true confessions. "Something like that."

He followed her. "I always said there was no one like you."

She remembered. But the effect had been tempered, because he meant it as a friend. "One of a kind," she agreed flippantly. "That's me."

He saw beyond the slightly lopsided smile. "Don't put yourself down, Caroline."

She wished he'd stop. Any second now, she was going to really make a mess of things. "I'm not. I'm agreeing with you. Can't you tell?"

He began to open the door, then stopped himself. He couldn't let her go just yet. Not without being honest. That was what their friendship was based on, honesty.

His eyes held hers. "What I can tell is that there's something going on between us." Sloan hesitated. "About the other night..."

She couldn't bear it if he was going to apologize again. She didn't want to hear him refer to one of the most special moments of her life as a mistake.

Caroline put her finger to his lips to keep him from saying anything else.

"You don't have to explain, Sloan. It was an accident. If I'd turned my head the other way, you would have gotten a mouthful of hair. It was a toss-up." She dropped her hand. "Luck of the draw."

There was something in her eyes, something he didn't understand. Something that matched the unsettled feeling he was experiencing. "Joey thinks your hair smells nice." He was fumbling, he thought.

She smiled warmly, relieved to be retreating to a safe area. "Joey's a great kid."

"Yeah, he is. And accurate. It does." If he concentrated, he could catch a little of the scent. It seemed only to disarm him further. Knowing it would be cowardly to stop now, he tried again. "Caroline, I'm not too sure what I'm feeling right now. Or if I'm really feeling anything at all, or just reacting, but—"

He'd nailed her, she thought. With that single word, with that single look, he had nailed her. Rendered her completely immobile.

"But?" she repeated, prodding him, knowing she'd probably regret it.

"Would you misunderstand if I kissed you right now?" He knew he wanted to, if only to prove to himself that the spark of electricity he felt the other night had just been the product of an overactive mind given to creativity. If asked, he would have sworn that he was completely dead inside, empty, save for the affection he bore his sons and his mother.

But what he'd experienced for a single moment that night with Caroline was calling him a liar. He wanted to prove it wrong.

She tried to make it easy for him. Heaven knew it was past that point for her. "'A kiss is just a kiss,' right?" she quoted.

Unless it comes from someone you've loved ever since you could remember, she added silently.

"Right," he agreed, feeling suddenly nervous without knowing why. "What's that from?"

"The theme song to *Casablanca*. Shame on you, everyone knows that."

It was the last thing she said before his lips touched hers.

Chapter 6

Sloan only meant for it to be an experiment.

A refutation—no, a denial—of the emotions he secretly, in the recesses of his soul, thought might be lingering somewhere within him, unattached. He meant only to brush his lips against hers again, the way he had before, and put an end to it.

That was how it began.

There was no refutation.

No disclaimer.

What had happened the other night happened again. The feeling returned, this time stronger for the anticipation fueling it. A second before he touched his mouth to hers, he knew it was coming. That same rush, that same surge.

Electricity crackled through his veins, as if he'd somehow been plugged into a high-powered outlet.

Stunned, Sloan drew his head away and looked at Caroline, unable to put his thoughts into anything that might remotely pass as coherent order. Afraid of recognizing what he thought he felt. Not without further proof.

But it was instinct, rather than logic, that pushed him to his next move. Subconscious instinct that took over the wheel of his pilotless plane.

Like a man walking through a dream, Sloan slipped his fingers through her hair, framing her face. Capturing it, capturing the moment and holding on to it in sheer wonder.

Caroline?

Every crevice of his brain echoed her name. How could he be feeling all this, whatever "this" was, about Caroline?

And yet he was.

Sloan pulled her to him without warning, perhaps even roughly, but there was no proper way to deal with what was going on inside of him. The lid had blown clean off, and he hadn't even known there was an explosion pending. Emotions ran pell-mell through him. It was as if a prisoner who had dwelled in solitary confinement for far too long had been suddenly released.

Hunger, need, desire, all battered his body, confusing the hell out of him. He would have sworn on a stack of Bibles that he was beyond all that.

Apparently, he'd been wrong.

Caroline could feel a buzzing in her head, a roaring in her ears. There was no floor below, and no ceiling above. And there was no holding back.

There were a thousand reasons she should hold back, several that sprang to mind immediately. Not one of them stood up. Not a one of them was strong enough to block the feelings that had lived within her for all these years, in secret or in plain sight.

She'd waited for this kiss all her life.

Reality did not pale in the face of anticipation. If anything, it was the other way around.

Her blood hummed his name.

Caroline wound her fingers through his hair. Her heart hammering so hard it threatened to break out of her chest, Caroline molded her body to his and lost herself in the timeless moment that a benevolent heaven had seen fit to grant her.

On her toes, she strained to draw in every ounce of sensation. The feel of his breath, the texture of his mouth, the warming imprint of his body along hers.

She wanted more.

She'd worked so hard at convincing herself that she didn't want this, but it had all been a lie, a sham. She did want it. With every fiber of her being.

It vaguely occurred to her that one of them should report this five-alarm fire before the house burned down around them.

Later.

There would be time for everything later. Right now, all she wanted was to stay here like this, absorbing every last nuance. Drowning in him. Dying happily.

The kiss grew deeper, fathomless, taking her in with it. She went willingly.

Caroline felt weak, strong, limp, invigorated. She could probably have recited the Chinese alphabet backward if anyone asked her to. There was nothing she couldn't do, nothing she couldn't conquer, now that the impossible had finally happened.

The hunger that had sprung out, full-blown, grew, holding on to Sloan so tightly he couldn't even draw a deep breath. Urges sprang to the foreground, demanding satisfaction.

He wanted to take her, heaven help him, he wanted

to make love with her all night. To rid himself of this overwhelming longing that wrenched his gut and had surprised him so completely.

Sloan could feel his hands trembling as he swept them along the length of her, losing himself in the scent, the taste, the feel of her. His head was swimming when he reached for the buttons on her blouse.

"Dad?"

The childish voice, infused with sleepiness and confusion, shattered the moment with the force of a fifteen-megaton bomb. Caroline and Sloan jumped back from each other, propelled away by the power contained within the small boy's presence.

Caroline blinked to clear her vision, if not the chaos in her mind. Danny was standing in the room, only a few feet away, staring at them.

How much had he seen? What was going on in his head?

She harnessed the unease that threatened her and crossed to him. "Is something wrong with Joey?"

With a clenched fist, Danny rubbed his eye. The lights in the room were too bright, after just his night-light and the dim light Dad always kept on in the hallway to chase away the monsters.

"No, I just came to tell you he was asleep." Danny looked up at his father. "I thought maybe you'd want to know."

It took effort to concentrate on what his son was saying. Effort to drag air back into his depleted lungs. The kiss had caught him completely off guard. He remembered getting into a fight once, when he was hardly more than Danny's age. He'd taken a sucker punch to his gut and gone down like a stone. That was what this felt like,

Sloan realized—as if he'd walked right into another sucker punch.

But there was no time to dwell on that now. From the looks of things, he needed to perform some damage control. Placing a hand on Danny's shoulder, he turned the boy around and pointed him toward the stairs.

"Thanks, I appreciate being told. You've done a good job." The words came out quickly, in a staccato rhythm. He just wanted Danny to go back to sleep. With any luck, in the morning the boy would think this was all part of a dream. And maybe, he considered, in a way it was. "Now go back to bed. There's school tomorrow."

Halting in his tracks, Danny looked up at his father, confused. "Tomorrow's Saturday, Dad."

Guilt sharpened his impatience. Danny shouldn't have seen this. More than that, *he* shouldn't have done this, Sloan thought, annoyed with himself.

"Well, there's morning tomorrow, I know that for sure. So get to bed," Sloan said curtly.

There was a hurt look in Danny's eyes as he retreated. Without another word, he turned away and hurried up the stairs.

Caroline waited until Danny disappeared. Once she was sure he was out of earshot, she planted herself directly in front of Sloan, so that he couldn't avoid looking at her.

She knew that guilt had prompted him, but that was no excuse. "You don't have to take it out on Danny."

Sloan's mouth hardened. "I'm not taking anything out on anyone."

She knew him too well to be taken in by a lie. "Oh, yes, you are."

He turned away, but she refused to be ignored. Though she still felt the same way about him, and always would, she was no longer the girl she had once been. Life would have plowed her under long ago if she hadn't changed.

Caroline placed her hands on his chest to keep him still. "You kissed me, Sloan, and now you feel guilty." Her eyes searched his face, and she knew she was right, no matter how much she hoped she wasn't. "There's no reason to feel guilty."

Guilt, desire, hell—it was all swirling through him until he didn't know which end was up.

"I don't know what I'm feeling." He bit off the words sharply.

He immediately regretted them, and regained control. She was right; he shouldn't have taken it out on Danny. And he shouldn't be taking it out on her. This was no one's fault but his. He took a deep breath, dragging his hand through his hair.

And then he said something he'd never admitted before. "I don't know, it's like I'm walking through a maze. I have been ever since she left me." The last part had just slipped out somehow. He cursed himself for it. But Caroline was the last person in the world he wanted to risk hurting. And he had just used her. "I just don't want you to think—"

She wouldn't let him finish. She'd had her moment, and she knew there wouldn't be another. She didn't want him ruining it with rhetoric that was laced with regret.

"I don't think anything." She saw the doubt in his eyes, as well as the torment. He was still haunted by his love, rather than comforted by it. Until the latter happened, he would have no peace. "And Julie didn't leave you, Sloan," she pointed out. "Leaving means making a choice. Julie didn't have a choice. She died." Her eyes held his. She didn't want him misunderstanding her motive, but he had to be made to see this. "And you didn't."

He hadn't talked about Julie since she died, not more than a word or two, and then only when cornered. It had been a defense mechanism, put in place so that he could survive, so he could outrace the pain before it could devour him. He didn't want to talk about her now, not even with Caroline. What was the point?

But Caroline was obviously waiting for a response. He gave it to her.

"I felt like I did die." He shoved his hands into his pockets, frustration getting the better of him. "Maybe I should have."

She could have hit him.

"And what?" Caroline demanded heatedly. "Left those boys orphans, just to ease your pain?"

Caroline waved an angry hand toward the stairs, emphasizing her question. He said nothing. With effort, she reined in her temper. She ached for him, for the pain she knew he had to be feeling. But sympathy wasn't what he needed. He needed to get on with his life. To finally lay Julie to rest in his heart.

"You know you don't mean that, Sloan. What about their pain? Danny and Joey lost a mother. I lost a dear, wonderful best friend." Caroline took his hands into hers, desperate to make him understand that he wasn't alone. "She touched all our lives for a reason. That reason is gone if you don't go on with your own life, Sloan, if you stop moving, stop growing. The boys need you."

His eyes grew dark. He wouldn't let her use his own sons to preach at him. What did she know about what it was like to lose someone she loved?

"Danny and Joey are the only reason I've been going on."

"Good." Caroline saw his eyes grow flinty. She steeled herself, making light of what had happened, even though it killed her to do it. But this was for him.

"Like I said, a kiss is just a kiss. Maybe that was just something you had to get out of your system, to see if you could still put your two lips together and make it count." Gathering her things together, she moved toward the door. "I promise I won't have a minister here in the morning."

Maybe she was right. He was just overreacting. "Sorry I yelled at you."

She shrugged it off. "Apology accepted."

Slowly, relief began to pour through him. "You're some terrific lady, you know that?"

Her mouth curved. He was going to be all right. In time. "That's what it says on my business cards—'Caroline Masters, M.D. and some pretty terrific lady.'" She patted his arm. "Now get some sleep, Sloan. You look like hell, and Joey's going to be pretty cranky tomorrow."

He nodded, opening the door for her. "Right." He watched as she began to walk toward her car. "Caroline?"

She turned, waiting.

"Thanks."

It didn't seem nearly enough, but she would understand. She always had before.

Caroline wondered what part he was most grateful for, her help with Joey, or the fact that she wasn't going to make anything of what had happened the other night and now. "Don't mention it. I'll be by to look in on Joey tomorrow morning."

She congratulated herself on making it into her car before her knees gave out completely.

Suddenly very weary, she rested her head on the steering wheel. More than a few seconds passed before she'd pulled herself together enough to start the car and drive away.

It took him forever to fall asleep that night. He'd known it would. In the dark, his feelings assailed him, jumping at him from all sides.

What had he been thinking? He had no business kissing Caroline like that. She was a friend and he needed her, but that was where it ended. He didn't want to jeopardize their friendship for some formless, nameless thing that he didn't understand. After over sixteen years, this was a hell of a time to let hormones come between them. He cared too much about Caroline to let anything physical get in the way of what they had.

But in the dark, the physical reaction he'd had to her, and the one she'd obviously had to him, grew large enough to almost engulf him.

The last time he looked at the clock, it was ten after two.

Normally, Sloan didn't dream, waking in the morning like someone emerging out of a void. Out of one void, into another. But tonight, fragments of a dream nudged their way forward in his subconscious.

Vivid fragments.

He was in school again. Julie was with him, looking just the way she always had, so vibrant and alive that his heart eagerly denounced her death as a lie.

Things fell into disjointed order. They were in high school, but she was asking after the boys. As he was trying to find Danny and Joey, Caroline walked up to them. She moved next to Julie and stood beside her. Then, before his eyes, their faces, so different from one another, began to merge in a macabre dance, interchanging until, finally, Julie's faded away completely.

There was only Caroline.

And then it was Caroline coming to him. Caroline who led him to the boys.

Caroline.

He woke with a start, sweating in spite of the cool temperature in the room. He could hear his heart pounding in his ears.

No, not his heart. The telephone. The telephone beside his bed was ringing. Who the hell could be calling him at this hour?

He wondered if his mother had hit the jackpot and was calling to tell him.

Taking a deep breath, uttering a ripe curse at the state of his nerves, Sloan groped for the receiver in the dark. With his other hand, he reached up to turn on the lamp.

"Hello?"

There was only silence on the other end of the line. Pregnant silence.

"Hello?" Listening, Sloan thought he heard someone breathing. Maybe something *was* wrong. He thought of his dream. "Caroline, is that you?"

The connection was abruptly cut off. A sharp click resounded in his ear.

Hell of a time to get a wrong number, he thought grumpily, dropping the receiver back in the cradle. He missed. Muttering under his breath, he reached for the receiver and tried again. Now he'd probably never get back to sleep.

But it was too early to get up. As he reached out to shut off the light, he saw the small figure standing in the doorway for the first time. The hall light made the figure look even smaller and more lost, somehow.

He thought it was Joey, but there was no cast. Sloan sat up and focused.

"Danny?" Slowly the head moved up and down in reply. "Phone wake you up, too?" This time the boy shook his head.

Sloan was about to ask what was wrong, but then it came to him. For all his bravado, Danny was the sensitive one, the one whose feelings were hurt most easily. And he had snapped at him earlier.

Feeling like a heel, Sloan drew back the light comforter on his bed. It was all the invitation Danny needed. The boy scurried over and climbed into bed.

Sloan tucked the comforter around his son. Danny sank back on the pillow. "Have a nightmare?"

Danny turned his head to look at him. His eyes looked wide and troubled. "No, I heard you moaning. It was a scary sound."

He tried to imagine what it was like to have the adult you depended on sound as if he were afraid. Pretty unnerving, probably.

"Sorry, sport." Sloan paused, then added, "For everything."

He understood. Danny accepted the apology. All was forgiven and forgotten instantly. Sympathy poured over his expressive face. "Did you have a nightmare?"

It hadn't been a nightmare, really, but what could it be called? Foreshadowing? Fear? Or the cumulative result of too much stress and tension without release? Danny was too young for a philosophical discussion. Sloan went with what was simplest.

"Kind of."

Danny sat up, peering at his dad's face. "Full of monsters?"

Danny loved to watch monster movies, but the result

was always the same. He'd spend weeks nervously eyeing his bedroom door at night, jumping every time there was an unidentified noise. His fears were at their apex in the winter, during the rainy season.

"You don't want to hear about it." Sloan was in no mood to try to make anything up, and the truth was far too confusing to launch into. He wasn't even sure he knew what the truth was in this case. "I thought you were supposed to keep an eye on Joey."

Danny lay back down, smoothing out the comforter carefully. "He's sleeping like a rock." He was echoing the phrase his father used.

"And you want to sleep here for the rest of the night?" It was a rhetorical question, he realized with a smile.

Danny looked hopefully up at his dad. "Just for a little while?" He knew it was pretty close to morning. But as long as it was dark outside, it was spooky inside without his dad around to guard him.

"Okay." Sloan turned on his side, away from Danny. "G'night, sport."

"G'night." There was silence, but not for long. "Dad?"

Maybe he should get up, Sloan reconsidered. It didn't look as if he were going to get much rest. "What?"

"Were you kissing Caroline in the living room?"

He hadn't seen that one coming.

Sloan's first inclination was to deny it, but it had been a kiss. What else could he call it? He'd always taught his sons not to lie. That way, he'd told them, he could always trust them, no matter what they said. But the road ran both ways. If he began lying to them, that would undermine the trust they had in him. He'd rather die than have that happen—no matter what kind of awkward position telling the truth placed him in.

"Yes."

Danny stared at his dad's back. "Why? Do you like her?"

Sloan turned around to face his son. It wasn't the kind of conversation that could be carried on with the wall.

"Sure, I like Caroline." He didn't want it to seem like a big deal. After all, it wasn't, really. Was it? "So do you."

"Yeah." Grinning, Danny cocked his head, thinking. "Can I kiss her like that?"

Could Danny have a crush on Caroline? The last thing he needed or wanted was for Danny to think they were involved in some sort of competition for her.

"You're too short."

The answer made sense to Danny, but it didn't put him off. "When I get taller, then can I?"

He was serious, wasn't he? Sloan propped himself up on his elbow and studied his son's face. "Since when did you start liking girls?"

Danny flushed. He knew it was like saying you liked eating liver or brussels sprouts if you said you liked girls. Lately, though, he didn't hate them quite as much as he used to. He especially didn't hate Cindy Tyler as much as he used to. She had a real pretty smile, and he liked the way her hair flew behind her when she ran in the play area during recess. But he didn't want anyone to know yet.

"I don't," he said vehemently. But his dad obviously did. He had kissed Caroline. Danny knew what he'd seen. "But Caroline's not a girl. She's special." When his father said nothing, Danny propped himself up on his elbow, mimicking Sloan. He looked up into his dad's eyes. "Right, Dad?"

There was no denying that. "Right." Sloan looked at the clock on the nightstand next to Danny's side of the bed. Four o'clock. He had a rehearsal scheduled in another five hours, and as of now, he'd had about two hours' sleep, tops.

He laid down the law for Danny. "Now close your eyes and your mouth and go to sleep, Danny, or I'll send you back to your room."

Danny did as he was told. Lying down flat, he squeezed his eyes shut tight. "They're closed."

Sloan laughed and gathered his son to him. He had enough right here and in the other room to fill his life completely.

There weren't going to be any more lapses, he promised himself.

"So how's my favorite patient doing?" Caroline asked as she came into the family room. When she rang the bell the next morning, it had been Danny, not Sloan, who let her in. Danny had brought her in to see Joey. She wondered whether things were going to become awkward between her and Sloan. She desperately hoped not.

She was here for Joey, not Sloan, she reminded herself. She placed the box she'd brought on the sofa.

"It hurts, but that's okay. It's supposed to—you said so." Joey eyed the wrapped box. "Is that for me?"

She pressed her lips together to hold back a smile. "It might be."

"It is for me," he declared excitedly. "What is it?"

She gestured at the box. "Why don't you open it and find out?"

She didn't have to tell him twice. Securing one side with his cast, he ripped into the paper.

"I'll help you," Danny volunteered.

"I can do it," Joey insisted. He didn't want to be treated like a baby. He was too fiercely independent for that.

His father's son, she thought. Not wanting any help, even when he needed it.

Tossing the paper aside, Joey looked at the gift. She'd brought him a board game. Caroline thought it was a safe bet that Joey, a child of the nineties, didn't have anything this simplistic.

"I thought that since you couldn't play any electronic games for a while, maybe you might like something a little old-fashioned."

His eyebrows puckered together as he studied the picture on the outside of the box. "Old-fashioned?"

"You have to move the pieces around by hand." No bells, no whistles, no dragons leaping out of cyberspace. Just sheer imagination and a handful of colorful playing pieces.

Joey pried off the lid, looking at the game board. Tiny single-colored figures resided in unopened plastic bags. There were four colors to choose from. "Did you ever play this?"

"Lots of times." It was the first game she remembered ever playing with her father. "When I was around your age."

That was good enough for him. He looked at her, his eyes shining. "Can you play with me?"

Sloan, who had been watching from a distance, entered the room. "Joey, Caroline doesn't have time to play."

Her heart did a little flip at the sound of his voice.

Steady. You promised to act as if nothing happened be-tween you. Instinctively she knew that was the only way their friendship could continue.

Caroline turned around with a smile. "How do you know what Caroline has time for?" she teased. "As it so happens," she informed the boys, "I'm free this morning. I don't go on duty for another four hours."

She might have time, but he didn't. "I'm afraid we have to get going as soon as you check Joey out. I called a rehearsal for this morning."

After what had happened last night? "And you're taking the boys with you?"

He knew what she was thinking, but he had no choice. "My mother's still gambling her heart out in Vegas, and I couldn't get a sitter." He'd been on the phone with everyone he knew this morning, but with no luck. Everyone was busy.

It took her only a second to make up her mind. "You just did."

"You?" Over her head, he saw his sons' faces light up. It would be the perfect solution, but he couldn't keep taking advantage of Caroline this way. Especially not after last night. "Caroline, I can't ask you."

"You didn't ask me," she pointed out. "I volunteered. Besides, I have to explain the rules of the game to Joey." She looked at him significantly. "I don't think you remember them well enough to teach him. So go, work with your thespians. I'll handle the small stuff."

She'd pushed him out the door before he could protest any further. As it shut behind him, he heard the sound of laughter. Caroline's, and then the boys.

Caroline knew how to take over, he thought as he walked to his car. She'd certainly changed a great deal since he knew her in school.

He was smiling as he turned on the ignition.

Chapter 7

His head nodding in time to the music the school orchestra was playing, Sloan smiled to himself. This was good. This was very good.

Today's rehearsal was going far more smoothly than yesterday's run-through had given him the right to hope for. It looked as if miracles did happen once in a while, he mused. Sloan gave himself little credit for the vast improvement he was seeing. He figured the speech he'd given them before Joey's accident had far less to do with the change than the fact that the students were trying to find a way of saying how concerned they all were about the boy. Joey and Danny had become the drama department's unofficial mascots.

At least something positive had come out of the scare, Sloan thought. He jotted down a note to himself about costumes. And now that Joey saw that there were consequences to behaving recklessly, maybe he'd think twice before doing something risky.

Then again, maybe not, Sloan mused, watching as Allison and the rest of the ensemble went into a rousing rendition of the finale. After all, look at Joey's old man. You'd think that a man who had gone through what he had would never think of even going out socially again.

Yet here he was...

Here he was, what? Sloan asked himself. Thinking of getting into an intimate relationship with Caroline? That was so absurd, he had no idea how the notion could have even occurred to him. Caroline would think he was crazy if he even so much as hinted at it.

Caroline was his friend, for heaven's sake. A *good* friend, and really good friends were hard to come by. What he had with Caroline was something he'd have to be out of his mind to consider jeopardizing.

And yet...

And yet he'd better get his mind back on what they were paying him such a nominal sum for, before the play began to suffer spasms of deterioration again. He knew the effect a lack of a positive feedback had. Hadn't he had teachers like that himself? Teachers who had made him want to flee school and studies as soon as the law legally allowed? Especially Old Man Cotton.

He'd almost dropped out of school when he reached sixteen, Sloan remembered, recalling how miserable he'd been, sitting in that English class, listening to Cotton ridicule his every answer in his slow, maddening southern drawl, until he thought he couldn't stand it anymore. It had been Caroline who talked him into staying and sticking it out.

His mouth curved. She'd come at him from all directions with statistics, examples and stories of dropouts with failed lives, until he agreed to take on Old Man Cotton and American Lit 2 purely out of self-defense.

And now look at him. He was an English teacher himself, and loving every minute of it.

He thought of the stack of test papers on his desk at home, waiting to be graded. Well, almost every minute. But it might not have turned out that way if he followed his impulse. Nobody had been able to talk him into staying in school, not his parents. Not even...

He let the thought go. What remained was the memory of Caroline patiently arguing with him. If not for Caroline, a big section of his life might have been missed.

If not for Caroline, he mused again.

Caroline. It always came back to Caroline.

He was smiling at her, Allison thought. That special smile that was meant only for her. All the hours she'd put in, practicing, going over lines until she could say them in her sleep, were worth it, just to see him look at her like that.

Her heart fluttered in hopeful anticipation as the last notes faded from the auditorium. She needed to find a way to arrange for the two of them to be alone. Mr. Walters needed to see that she wasn't like the other girls. That she was a woman. Woman enough for him.

She smiled back at him, wishing he could read minds. He might as well, seeing as how hers belonged to him. As did the rest of her. He had only to reach out to take her.

Mr. Walters—no, not Mr. Walters, Sloan. Sloan. You couldn't be in love with someone and call him Mr. Walters, it didn't sound right. And she was so in love with him she could hardly stand it.

"Mr. Walters?"

Sloan blinked, rousing himself. He realized from Matt Prescott's expression that this wasn't the first time the lanky teenager had called his name. He leaned forward, his hands resting against the back of the seat in the row in front of him.

"Yes?"

"Is the finale okay, or do you want us to do it again?" Murmurings behind him followed the question. The rest of the cast obviously didn't want to tamper with what they perceived as their best.

Sloan rose, weaving through the third row until he came into the aisle.

"'Okay?'" he repeated, putting the right spark of enthusiasm in his voice. He didn't have to force it. "It's much more than okay."

He walked down the aisle, stopped just before the center of the stage and looked up at the students. They were a great bunch of kids, all of them. And he was grateful to be working with them, long hours notwithstanding.

"It's fantastic. You do the finale just like that the night of the play, and you're going to knock everyone's socks off."

Matt rubbed his shock of black hair. "Is that good?"

Allison looked at him haughtily, disgusted by his limited knowledge. She'd once foolishly thought herself in love with Matt. Now she poked him in the ribs.

"Of course it's good." She offered Sloan her best smile as she nimbly got off the stage. "Mr. Walters wouldn't say it if it wasn't." Moving closer to Sloan, Allison lowered her voice and raised her eyes to his face. "Did you get my flowers?"

"Yes, I did. Joey appreciated them, thank you." He looked at the others. He could feel the charged energy. Good rehearsal or not, they were all eager to get back to their Saturday lives, as far away from school as they could get.

He didn't blame them. He'd felt just like that at their age. "Okay, people, you're free."

Allison laced her fingers together behind her back, rocking on the balls of her feet. "I thought that maybe you...um..." Straightening, she squared her shoulders and stuck her chest out provocatively. "Do you need any help at home? You know, with Joey being hurt and all, you might..."

He caught the glimmer in her eye, and it made him slightly uncomfortable. Her enthusiasm was why he had picked her for the role of Annie Oakley, but he was getting the uneasy feeling that maybe some of that enthusiasm was being misdirected.

"Thanks for offering, Allison, but everything's under control." An idea occurred to him. "Tell you what you can do, though."

"Yes?" The word tumbled from her full, red-lined lips breathlessly.

He lowered his head, speaking softly, so that he wouldn't be overheard. Ever mindful of his experience with Old Man Cotton, Sloan didn't want to unnecessarily hurt anyone's feelings. "See if you can infuse a little of your energy into Matt. His Frank Butler is good, but it's not up to your standards. Maybe you could work with him."

He was sharing a confidence with her, she thought gleefully, his breath warm on her cheek and in her heart. Allison could have thrown her arms around Sloan's neck, but there were still too many people around. It would mean his job if they were caught, and if he lost that, his pride would suffer. But she still chafed to touch him.

Restraining herself, Allison looked over her shoulder toward Matt. The full weight of Sloan's words sank in.

He wanted her to work with Matt, to spend time with him. Time she'd rather spend with Sloan. Or at least daydreaming about him.

She frowned. "I'll try."

Had he gotten his stories mixed up? "What's the matter? I thought you and Matt were an item, that you were going together."

"We are—I mean were." She meant to break it off with Matt as soon as she found the right words. After all, a woman couldn't go with one man if she loved another. "But..." Once again, she raised her blue eyes up at him, in what Sloan thought was the most calculating manner he'd ever seen. "He's just such a kid, Mr. Walters."

"He is a kid, Allison," he pointed out, doing his best not to laugh at her protest. She sounded like a world-weary Faye Dunaway.

Allison smiled in triumph. They were in agreement. "Exactly. And I like, you know, more mature men." She drew as close to him as she dared on school property. You never knew when the principal might turn up.

She was vamping him, Sloan thought, stunned. With her firm young breasts all but pressed against him, and that come-hither look in her eyes, she was vamping him. No question about it.

Caroline was right.

Caroline, he was beginning to think, was always right about things.

For all concerned, Sloan tried to keep it as light as possible as he slipped his script and the notes he'd made today into his briefcase.

"Give him time, Allison. He'll catch up." Out of the corner of his eye, he could see Matt watching them. Did the teenager see him as a threat to his romance with Allison? How the hell had this happened? And when?

Allison raised her chin. "Maybe I don't want him to catch up."

Sloan purposely put distance between them. Allison obviously didn't seem to be affected by the fact that there were other students around and that, any second now, they might be attracting attention.

"Oh, I don't know. Matt might be worth the wait. We guys tend to fumble and trip over our own feet at that age, but it all works out in the end."

"You were never like that," she insisted.

She was in far too much of a rush to grow up, he thought. Why did that seem so familiar? Sloan laughed. "I would have made Matt look like Cary Grant."

Allison shook her head, lost. Her carefully curled long hair tumbled over her shoulders as she cocked her head. "Who?"

He had to remember that not everyone loved old movies the way he did. "An actor who was known for his suaveness and sophistication."

She didn't care about ancient history. All she cared about was the here and now. And Sloan. "I don't believe it. Not you."

"Believe it." He snapped the locks on his briefcase, closing it. Closing their conversation, too. He swung the briefcase off the empty seat. "Now, if you'll excuse me, I've got to be getting home." He put more distance between them before she could think of an excuse to tag along. "Great job, guys," he said to the few stragglers who still remained as he took his leave. "Don't forget, Tuesday. Five-thirty. Right here. You're all making me proud of you."

He left quickly, before Allison could think to catch up to him.

When he walked into his house twenty minutes later, he was still trying to figure out how he had managed to remain oblivious to Allison's advances. Rethinking the past few weeks, he realized that he must have gone around in blinders. His only excuse was that he'd had too much on his mind. As usual.

Caroline was sitting cross-legged on the rug in the family room. Joey sat across from her, and the game board was between them. Danny rounded out the picture. There were several abandoned bowls on the coffee table, each with telltale streaks of brown, indicating that they had recently been filled with chocolate ice cream.

"Hi. Welcome back." Caroline glanced up at him. Sloan had a strange expression on his face. "What's up?"

Sloan perched on the arm of the sofa. It sagged a little, reminding him that he'd been meaning to look into buying a new one. "You were right."

She took the observation as her due. "Of course I was. About what?" She grinned when Joey giggled. He had the most infectious laugh. Hearing it made her want to laugh, too.

"Allison. I think she has a crush on me." Did that sound as pompous as he thought it did?

Joey was moving his blue piece several squares across the board. With the greatest of glee, he knocked away the yellow piece in his path with the one he was holding, sending it flying.

"Gotcha!" he needlessly announced to Caroline, then looked up at his father. "What's a crush?"

Sloan looked positively embarrassed, she thought.

"That's when someone likes someone else a whole bunch," she told Joey.

"Like Dad likes you?" Danny asked.

"Not exactly," Caroline said quickly, in her estimation sparing Sloan the trouble.

But Danny knew he'd gotten it right. "But he said he did." His eyes shifted to his father for support. "Didn't ya, Dad? In bed last night."

"You got to sleep with Dad last night?" Joey pouted, his victory a thing of the past. "Hey, I was the hurt guy."

The truce between the brothers was definitely over. "You were sleeping like a rock," Danny said haughtily.

Joey scrambled up to his knees. "Was not. Rocks don't sleep, do they, Caroline?"

She wasn't about to take sides. "Hey, no arguing, guys. Let me remember you peacefully." Holding her hands up before her face, she formed a frame and pretended to capture them within its borders. "Okay, I've got it. Now, I have to go."

"Aw, Caroline." In a flash, Joey was on his feet. "Just one more game," he pleaded.

She wasn't going to be coerced, even if he did have his father's eyes.

"Sorry, honey. Maybe you can convince your dad to play with you. It's time for me to go to work." She glanced at her watch. "My shift starts in less than an hour." And she still wanted to go home and change. "There's just enough time to clean up."

"We can clean up for you," Danny volunteered. He grabbed his bowl, then reached for hers before Joey could get it. He held it up over his head in triumph, lording it over his brother.

"You're cleaning up for your dad," Caroline pointed out as they raced each other for the kitchen.

His sons were actually fighting to see who cleaned up. "How *do* you do that?" Sloan asked, marveling.

She rose to her feet, dusting off her knees. "Magic. That, and I bribed them with a half-gallon container of chocolate mousse ice cream."

She had the tiniest dab at the corner of her mouth. He saw it now that she'd turned her head in his direction. Without thinking, he reached over and rubbed it off with his thumb. "I was going to ask where that came from."

She felt that same ripple she'd felt before. The same one that came every time he touched her. She had as much hope of being with Sloan as Allison did, she thought, momentarily feeling sorry for the girl. "There's a little left in the fridge. Sorry, I couldn't resist."

Resist. It was all he could do to resist finding out whether there was any residual taste of chocolate on her lips.

Where the hell had that come from? And why was it still here, growing stronger by the minute? What was the matter with him, anyway?

Sloan shoved his hands into his pockets, knowing that any second they would be invaded by Danny and Joey. He didn't want to have to explain about kissing Caroline again.

Caroline could feel the tension building within her. If she didn't keep a tight rein on herself, she was going to do something stupid. Like kiss him. She drew in a deep breath and let it out again. "So, what are you going to do about her?"

"Her?" he repeated, watching the light play off her lips.

"Your groupie. Allison."

He shrugged. "Hope she gets over it soon. In the meantime, stay out of dark alleys, in case she tries to corner me." His grin faded a little. "How did you know? About Allison. I mean, I didn't, and I was right there."

Caroline laughed. "Because, my friend," she said, brushing her hand along his cheek, "you can be so dense about these things."

He caught her hand. Was he imagining it, or was she alluding to something else? "Really?"

A warm feeling spiraled through her. "Sure, there are probably legions of budding femmes fatales in your school, all doodling their initials with yours instead of listening to their geometry teacher." *Like I did.*

That was what she was talking about. His students. For a moment, he'd thought she was talking about— When had his ego gotten so large?

And then her words registered. He groaned. "I just might have to hire you for protection."

"To scare them off? Dr. Caroline Masters strikes fear into the hearts of young, impressionable teenage girls. Like a human scarecrow." Amusement danced across her face. "Thanks a lot."

He shook his head. "No, like a gorgeous girlfriend they didn't have a prayer of competing with."

She pressed her lips together to keep her slackened jaw from dropping. It took her a second to recover. "Why, Sloan Walters, that was a very nice thing to say."

He winked at her. "I have my moments." He heard dishes clattering in the background. The boys were probably trying to load the dishwasher. He hoped nothing had gotten broken. Or worse. He wasn't up to another run to the emergency room.

She didn't hear the noise. She wasn't aware of anything except Sloan. "Yes," she agreed quietly, "you do."

He linked his hand with hers. "Do you really have to go?" He wasn't ready to explore any new emotional territory just yet; all he knew was that he liked having Caroline around. That the boys were nicer, situations easier to take, less confusing, less maddening, when she was with them. "I thought maybe you could, you know, stick around for a while." He shrugged, searching for a way to entice her. "Maybe we could take in a movie or something. The boys and you and I." There was safety in numbers and he felt as if he still needed that safety factor for now. "They're playing *Sam Did It* in the Deerborn Complex, just a couple of miles away."

She liked being included in his plans. Liked being included, period. She wished she could take him up on it, but she had to go. Maybe she shouldn't have allowed Dr. Wiseman to talk her into taking the temporary position at the hospital.

Temporary was the key word, she reminded herself. All of this was just temporary.

But even if it was, she wanted to make the most of it.

Reluctantly she withdrew her hand. "I know where the complex is, and it's a very tempting offer, but I really do have to go to the hospital. How would it look, skipping out on my second day there?"

Sloan nodded. It was for the best. He was beginning to feel awkward about the invitation, anyway. He didn't want Caroline to think he was coming on to her.

What else could she think?

And what was he doing, really, if not coming on to her?

When the hell had life gotten this damn fouled up?

"But I'm off Sunday." Was she being pushy? Well, why not? She was tired of being passive. "Maybe then?"

He nodded, not really knowing what to make of the contented feeling that her words stirred. "The guys'll like that."

They were waltzing around, using his sons as buffers, she thought. "Wouldn't want to disappoint the guys."

As if by magic, the boys materialized, running in to flank her like animated bookends. "We put the dishes in the dishwasher," Joey crowed.

She slipped one arm around his shoulders. "That was very nice of you."

Danny nudged himself under her other arm. "Can you come back tonight?"

"Yeah, please?" Joey pleaded. They both put on long, sad faces, turning them first toward Caroline, then toward their father.

Sloan found it hard not to laugh. "Guys, don't bother Caroline."

"We're not bothering her," Danny said indignantly. "We're telling her we like her being around."

"A girl always likes to hear that." She couldn't resist looking at Sloan. Then she turned her attention back to her cheering section. "But maybe your dad has other plans."

Danny shook his head at the objection. "Dad never has plans, right, Dad?"

That made him sound like a pitiful recluse, he thought. Was that how they saw him?

"Right." He looked at Caroline, adding to his sons' invitation. "Why don't you come? I'll even try to whip up something."

He had to be kidding. "Emphasis on the word *whip?*" Caroline shuddered. "Thanks, but the only way you'll get me to come back for dinner is if I'm in charge of it. No offense."

So now she was making fun of his culinary efforts, too. And she'd never had to sample any. Still, he couldn't very well argue that he knew his way around a kitchen.

"None taken." He had to raise his voice to be heard above his sons' very lusty cheers.

All three of them escorted her to the front door. Danny even held it open for her.

"See you." She turned to look at them standing in the doorway.

They made quite a picture, she mused, framed by the doorway like that. She would have given anything if that picture belonged to her.

There she went again, wishing for the impossible. Things would remain fine as long as she remembered her place. And that place was in a little niche labeled Friend. Not Girlfriend, not Lover, just Friend. She knew what could happen if she got greedy. She could lose it all.

She wasn't prepared to risk that. In the final analysis, she wasn't a risk-taker.

Sloan hadn't thought he could really enjoy a movie aimed at the seven-year-old mind. He never had before. But somehow, having Caroline there with them made the difference. So much so that he hadn't even dozed off in the middle of the movie, the way he normally did. He couldn't doze off, not with Caroline sitting there.

True, she did have one of his sons on either side of her, an arrangement that had taken over five minutes of

the boys arguing back and forth to arrive at. Lucky thing
they'd been the only ones in the theater until just before
the movie began. Each boy wanted to monopolize Caroline. He might as well not have come, for all the attention Joey and Danny had initially paid him.

He didn't mind. He liked watching them have a good
time.

Then, too, sitting here in the dark, it felt almost as if
they were part of a family again. A whole family, with
the prescribed number of participants. That was when
he'd been happiest, he thought. And that was why he
resisted whenever one of his friends suggested fixing
him up with someone. He didn't want to be fixed up.
He wasn't meant to be a single guy, out on the prowl.
He was a family man. A husband.

A husband, he reminded himself, without a wife.
Without the latter, he didn't qualify as the former.

Nothing he could do about that, he thought, watching
the lights from the screen play off Caroline's profile.

Wasn't there? a small voice whispered from the corners of his mind.

After the movie, they went for the obligatory ice
cream sundae and then home, where the boys coerced
Caroline into playing several more rounds of the game
she'd bought Joey. A few hours stretched into half a day.
Before he realized it, most of Sunday had passed and he
was walking her to her car again.

A pattern was beginning to emerge, he thought wryly.
One he could easily learn to live with.

"The boys really appreciate your going to the movies
with them." He was fumbling, he thought. But what he
wanted to say didn't feel as if it would come out right.
"And all the attention you've been giving them."

She smiled. She could honestly say that these past few days had been the best she could remember. "It's not hard—they're neat kids."

He shrugged, feeling as if his tongue weighed half a ton. "All the same, they appreciate it."

And you, Sloan. Do you appreciate it, too? She couldn't ask, even though she wanted to. Consequences again.

"My pleasure." She reached for her car door.

His hand went over hers. She looked up at him questioningly. He took a chance. "Look, I know it's late, and I don't want to keep you, but do you remember Mary Jenkins?"

She stared at him. He wanted to reminisce? Now?

"The geometry teacher?"

He nodded.

"Sure, I remember her." A thin, sad faced woman who had been completely dedicated to her subject and her students. There had been rumors that she had some great tragedy in her background. "What about her?"

"They're having a retirement party for her next week, and I was wondering if you'd like to come." He'd found a folded flyer discreetly placed in his In box at school Saturday morning, just before he walked into rehearsal. He'd been debating asking Caroline since then.

"Retirement? I thought she retired years ago." Caroline pictured the woman in her mind. "She was a hundred and three when we had her."

"Not quite." He laughed. "She turned sixty-five just before Christmas. The board of ed wanted her to retire then, but she talked them into the extra semester." The principal had gone to bat for her, not wanting to start a search for a geometry teacher in the middle of the school year. Replacing someone of Mrs. Jenkins's caliber was not an easy thing. "They're planning a big free-for-all party for her just before the end of the school year. Diane Palmetto is sending out invitations to as many of Mrs. Jenkins's old students as she can locate," he said, referring to the school secretary. "This party is just for faculty members."

Then why was he asking her to attend? "I'm not faculty."

"No, but you'd be my..." Sloan fumbled, getting his tongue around the word. "Date, I guess."

She was silent for a moment. "I've never been a 'date-I-guess' before." She looked at him impishly. "Any special rules I have to follow? Like walking ten paces behind you?"

She made him laugh. That was her gift, he thought. She brought laughter into his life. "Five'll do."

Caroline gave the thought some consideration. "Make it three and you've got yourself a deal. Do I bring anything?"

"Just yourself." He'd already put in twenty dollars to cover his share when the party was in the planning stages. He watched moonlight play off her hair, making it a soft golden brown. "You know, she always liked you."

Teachers had always liked her. The other students had rubbed her nose in that all through high school. "Why not? I was a teacher's dream. I actually wanted to learn."

He nodded, remembering his own study habits. "Not like the rest of us."

"No, not like the rest of you," she agreed quietly. "I was always on the outside, looking in." She didn't know what had made her say that.

He looked at her in surprise. He'd always thought of

her as part of his circle. "It didn't seem like that way to us."

"That's because you were on the inside." *And far too involved with one another to see any farther than your hearts.* "I never quite fit in back then."

Things had changed. She no longer hung back, no longer stayed on the sidelines. She had Julie to thank for that. Julie, who by example and by word had always pushed her to the foreground, always tried to make her have fun, no matter what she did. They'd been the original odd couple, she and Julie. Julie had been vivacious, outgoing, the center of every event, while she had been just the opposite. Only Julie hadn't let her, chipping away at her until she began to change on her own.

Maybe she hadn't fit in then, but she did now, Sloan thought. She fit in very well.

As she slid in behind the steering wheel, Sloan crouched down beside her. "Caroline, can I see you again?" he asked impulsively.

Her pulse quickened, but she refused to let herself get carried away and misinterpret his words. "Sure. I thought we just made a 'date-I-guess.'"

Suddenly he knew that wasn't enough. He wanted more. "I mean alone. Without a cheering section or a party to run interference."

"Sure," she repeated, her mouth going dry. She looked into his eyes and saw something she couldn't quite identify. Or was afraid to, in case she was wrong. But she had to ask, "Ready to take off the training wheels?"

"Yeah, I think so." He flushed ruefully, momentarily embarrassed. But this was Caroline. Caroline, to whom he could say anything. "I might land on my butt."

That makes two of us. "We'll work something out."

He skimmed his fingers over her hair. "How is it that you understand, Caroline? Without me explaining anything, you understand."

Because I've waited forever to hear you say this. "Haven't you heard? Mind reading is one of my specialties. Now go back inside before one of your sons hops out of bed and comes looking for you."

"Right." Before getting up, he leaned over and kissed her. Quickly. Sweetly. And found she still managed to take his breath away. "Tomorrow night? Seven?"

"Seven'll be fine." Had those calm words just come out of her mouth? She had more control than she'd thought she did.

Sloan rose to his feet. "I'll see you."

Count on it, she thought.

Chapter 8

She had a date with Sloan.

Humming, Caroline walked into her parents' house and dropped her purse on the hall table. Who would ever have thought that—

Her thoughts stopped abruptly. Her mother was standing by the window, dressed for bed, her face as pale as the beige fabric that hung loosely off her thin body.

An uneasy feeling undulated through her. This was late for her mother.

Caroline bent over to brush her lips across her mother's cheek. "Hi, what are you doing up?"

Wanda knotted her fingers together. She looked, Caroline thought, like a rabbit that didn't know which way to run. "Waiting for your father."

The last of her smile faded from Caroline's lips. It was past eleven o'clock. Her father liked to go to bed early these days. He'd been a morning person all his life, and his habit of rising early had only intensified since he retired.

Caroline was almost afraid to ask. "Why? Where is Dad?"

Fidgeting, Wanda shifted toward the window again. She pulled back the curtain behind the drape to look out on the street, the way she had done a hundred times in the past few hours. There wasn't even the faint glimmer of oncoming headlights to give her any false hope.

Nerves pricked at her with razor-sharp daggers. "He went out to pick up a box of doughnuts. You know how crazy he is about chocolate glazed doughnuts. You're just like him, you know. Loving chocolate the way you do. That's where you get it from. Your father."

Still there were no headlights breaking the darkness on the street, no cars announcing themselves in the distance. Wanda let the curtain fall again.

Her mother was rambling. Fear began clawing at Caroline's throat. "When did he leave?"

Wanda looked at the clock on the mantel. She didn't have to. The faint tick had resounded in the empty house, marking the passage of every minute for her, since her husband drove away.

"Two and a half hours ago."

It didn't take two and a half hours to cross the length of Bedford and return, much less go to any one of the shopping centers that were scattered through it.

Another thought assailed her. Caroline bracketed her mother's shoulders with her hands, forcing her to look at her.

"He drove the car?" There was a small shopping center on the other side of the development. He could have walked there, but even that wouldn't have taken two and a half hours.

Her mother nodded.

Caroline stared at her incredulously. What had her mother been thinking? "And you just let him go?"

Wanda twisted her fingers together, pressing them to her lips to keep back a sob. Helpless tears glistened in her eyes. She had wanted to stop him, had asked, almost begged, him to forget about the doughnuts and stay with her. But he hadn't listened.

"What was I to do," she demanded defensively, "take his car keys away from him?"

Didn't her mother realize just how serious her father's condition could be? What if he blacked out? Had a dizzy spell?

"Yes." Caroline's voice rose. "You should have taken his car keys away from him."

In her heart, Wanda knew her daughter was right. But this was so much more complicated than simple right and wrong. There was a man's pride to think of. Without that, she knew, he would fall apart.

Wanda tried to calm down and failed. Fear wouldn't let her. "I couldn't do that, Caroline. He's a very proud man."

Her mother couldn't possibly be so dense, so blind to consequences. She just couldn't be.

"I know that, but would you rather have him proud and dead, or annoyed and alive?" Caroline pressed her lips together. "I'm sorry, I didn't mean to shout at you."

"I thought he'd be all right." Wanda's voice was barely above a whisper. And even so, it trembled. "He's never had any trouble driving before."

It was a plea, a prayer that he was safe now, too. She'd been here, alone, worrying, sick at heart, haunted by the same ugly thoughts that she knew were spawning in her daughter's mind.

"He never forgot to pay the bills or what his favorite meal was before, either." Caroline shut her eyes, trying to think, trying to be positive.

Where could he be? She hadn't heard any sirens on her way home, but that was small consolation. Bedford wasn't the little three-traffic-light town it had once been. It hadn't been for years. And there were two freeways running through it. If her father had gotten on either one of them, he could be anywhere by now.

Fighting panic, Caroline hurried over to the wall phone in the kitchen.

Wanda followed quickly, her robe flapping against her legs. Catching Caroline by the arm, she turned her around. "Where are you going?"

Caroline struggled to sound calm. She was the one who set the pace. If she remained calm, she could assuage the rising panic in her mother's eyes.

When had she become the parent and her mother the child?

"To call the police. If I give them a description of Dad's car and the license plate number, maybe they'll find him and bring him home." *Before anything bad happens to him.*

Her mother stared into her eyes. It was as if she could read her mind. "Do you really think something's happened to him?"

Somehow, she managed an encouraging smile. "Probably not."

There was no doubt in Caroline's mind that her father had suffered one of his lapses. Best case, he'd just lost his way, or he'd forgotten where he was going and was too embarrassed to return. Worst case, he'd forgotten who he was.

No, that wasn't the worst case, Caroline thought.

How to validate your
Editor's FREE GIFT "Thank You"

1. Peel off gift seal from front cover. Place it in space provided at right. This automatically entitles you to receive two free books and a fabulous mystery gift.

2. Send back this card and you'll get brand-new Silhouette Intimate Moments* novels. These books have a cover price of $4.25 each, but they are yours to keep absolutely free.

3. There's no catch. You're under no obligation to buy anything. We charge nothing—ZERO—for your first shipment. And you don't have to make any minimum number of purchases—not even one!

4. The fact is thousands of readers enjoy receiving books by mail from the Silhouette Reader Service™. They like the convenience of home delivery...they like getting the best new novels BEFORE they're available in stores... and they love our discount prices!

5. We hope that after receiving your free books you'll want to remain a subscriber. But the choice is yours— to continue or cancel, any time at all! So why not take us up on our invitation, with no risk of any kind. You'll be glad you did!

6. Don't forget to detach your FREE BOOKMARK. And remember...just for validating your Editor's Free Gift Offer, we'll send you THREE gifts, *ABSOLUTELY FREE!*

GET A **FREE** MYSTERY GIFT..

YOURS FREE!

SURPRISE MYSTERY GIFT
COULD BE YOURS **FREE**
AS A SPECIAL
"THANK YOU" FROM
THE EDITORS OF SILHOUETTE

The Editor's "Thank You" Free Gifts Include:
- ● Two BRAND-NEW romance novels!
- ● An exciting mystery gift!

PLACE
FREE GIFT
SEAL
HERE

YES!
I have placed my Editor's "Thank You" seal in the space provided above. Please send me 2 free books and a fabulous mystery gift. I understand I am under no obligation to purchase any books, as explained on the back and on the opposite page.

245 SDL CF3Z   (U-SIL-IM-03/98)

Name

Address   Apt.

City

State   Zip

Thank You!

DETACH AND MAIL CARD TODAY!

The Silhouette Reader Service™ – Here's How It Works:

Accepting free books places you under no obligation to buy anything. You may keep the books and gift and return the shipping statement marked "cancel." If you do not cancel, about a month later we will send you 6 additional novels, and bill you just $3.57 each plus 25¢ delivery per book and applicable sales tax, if any.* That's the complete price, and—compared to cover prices of $4.25 each—quite a bargain! You may cancel at any time, but if you choose to continue, every month we'll send you 6 more books, which you may either purchase at the discount price...or return to us and cancel your subscription.
*Terms and prices subject to change without notice. Sales tax applicable in N.Y.

BUSINESS REPLY MAIL

FIRST-CLASS MAIL   PERMIT NO. 717   BUFFALO, NY

POSTAGE WILL BE PAID BY ADDRESSEE

SILHOUETTE READER SERVICE
3010 WALDEN AVE
PO BOX 1867
BUFFALO NY 14240-9952

NO POSTAGE
NECESSARY
IF MAILED
IN THE
UNITED STATES

There was something worse than that that could have happened to her father, but she wasn't going to deal with that now. She couldn't. And neither, she knew, could her mother. From the look on her face, her mother couldn't deal with any more than she was right now.

"Maybe he just ran into someone he knew and the time slipped away from him."

Her mother clutched at the flimsy excuse as if it were a life preserver in a stormy sea. "Maybe."

Caroline began to pick up the receiver. The telephone rang beneath her hand. She yanked it up as if it were red-hot.

Oh, please, let it be Dad. "Hello?"

"Caroline?"

The sigh of relief that whooshed through her took all the air from her lungs. She dragged some back in, offering a quick prayer of thanks. She held the receiver with both hands, afraid of dropping it. Caroline nodded in answer to the urgent question in her mother's eyes.

"Dad, where are you?"

Wanda tugged on her arm, blinking back tears. "Ask him if he's all right."

"Mom wants to know if you're all right."

The voice on the other end of the line was weary, very weary. "I suppose as all right as..." His voice trailed off for a second, then returned again. "I'm at a shopping center, Caroline." Shuffling noises followed. Had he dropped the receiver?

"Dad? Dad, are you there?" Tension cut through her like a sword, making small holes.

More noise. "Yes, I'm here." His voice became stronger as he spoke into the mouthpiece. "I was just looking to see if I could see a name for this place. It looks like Heritage Shopping Center. I..."

The agony he felt wafted through the telephone. She had no time for words of comfort. She had to get to him before something made him take off.

"Stay put, Dad. I'm coming to get you." She hesitated. She hated treating him like a child, but there was no other way open to her. "Promise me you won't go anywhere."

"I promise."

She heard the defeat in his voice. Caroline hung up. God willing, he'd keep that promise. He wasn't far. At this time of night, it shouldn't take her more than five minutes to get there.

"Do you want me to come with you?"

She'd almost forgotten about her mother. Caroline turned to look at her. She wasn't dressed, and Caroline didn't want to waste any time waiting for her. Besides, she had a feeling that her mother would rather not see him like this. "No, I think maybe this'll go easier if I go alone."

Wanda nodded, relieved. She squeezed her daughter's hand. "Thank you, Caroline."

Caroline understood, and ached for both her parents. "Why don't you make some hot chocolate for him? Put in a dash of amaretto."

A smile, half hopeful, half sad, rose to Wanda's lips. "His favorite."

"His favorite," Caroline echoed. *If he hasn't forgotten,* she added silently.

The shopping center was less than three miles from where her parents lived. It had been one of the first to be built in Bedford, and had been remodeled and restructured three times, to Caroline's recollection, in the past twenty years. Each time, a few more stores were added, a few more feet of open land eaten up. If her father did have Alzheimer's and he came here looking for the shopping center that lived in his memory, he would have gotten confused easily.

Is that what happened, Dad? Did you come here looking for the place we used to go to when I was a little girl? Did you panic when it wasn't here?

She turned into the shopping center using a side street that led directly to the bakery, one of the few staple factors that had remained through all the remodelings. It was right next to the pizzeria. Both were favorite haunts of her father's.

When she didn't see him in front of either, she felt heartsick.

Because of the hour, there were only a few cars scattered here and there. Huge street lamps hanging their Brobdingnagian heads kept the dormant stores company, lighting a way for anyone who was intent on a solitary late-night stroll. It was a long block that housed over two dozen stores and half that many parking lots, one interconnecting with another.

He had to be here somewhere.

Save for the shadows and the distance, Caroline's view was basically unobstructed. She drove slowly, picking her way from one end of the center to the other. Searching.

"Where are you, Dad?" There was nothing but the beating of her heart to keep her company. She'd shut off the radio because it interfered with her concentration. "Oh, please, Dad, don't have gone wandering off again. I can't bear this. I really can't."

And then she saw him.

A lonely figure standing by the hood of his car. He looked so lost.

Caroline stepped on the gas, going faster than she normally would in this area. But there were no shoppers to worry about, no children popping out from between parked cars. Despite the few cars, it was completely deserted. There were a discount shop devoted to anything made out of denim and a foreign car parts store at this end. Both had long since closed their doors for the night.

She pulled up beside her father's car, searching for the right thing to say. Nothing came to her. Nothing, except how much she loved this man that fate was treating so cruelly.

Caroline wanted to throw her arms around him, but she approached cautiously, almost afraid of what she would see when she looked into his face. He didn't seem to hear her.

"Daddy?"

Joshua Masters looked up. She was relieved to see that his eyes were clear. No befuddled look lurking there. Only a glimmer of self-loathing.

"I got lost," he told her, shaking his head. He looked around, as if surprised by his own words. "I've lived in this city all my life. Been involved in building a quarter of the shopping centers and a tenth of the homes that have gone up, and I got lost." His eyes turned toward her, helplessness, frustration and anger all fighting for equal parts of him. "What's happening to me, Carrie?"

And then she did put her arms around him. Held him, when she really wanted to be held instead. She wanted to bury her head in his chest, to cry because this wasn't fair. Not to him, not to any of them. He wasn't supposed to have something like this happen to him. He was her pillar, her strength, the man she had always thought would go on forever. He wasn't supposed to get sick, wasn't supposed to crumble before her eyes like a small, lost child.

But this wasn't the time to think of what she wanted. He was her father, and he needed her. That was all that mattered right now.

"That's what we're trying to find out, Daddy." Releasing him, she said, "We should have some word back on the tests tomorrow." He should have taken the tests earlier, but there was no point in bringing that up now. It was in the past.

Joshua nodded, but the hopelessness refused to leave his eyes. Instead, it grew, festering. "I know." He looked down into her face, searching for her strength, wanting to tap into it and ashamed because he did.

He felt cold. "I'm afraid, Carrie. For the first time in my life, I'm afraid."

It had to cost him, admitting that. She wanted to spare him, yet she knew that he needed to voice his fears out loud. And her mother, for all her love, would never listen.

"I know, Daddy, I know. But I'm here. And I'm staying here."

Surprise and hope rushed in. "You're moving back home?"

She nodded. "For as long as you need me."

That sounded temporary, he thought. Not that he could blame her. She was young. She had a life. But fear, black and threatening, made him ask. "And if I keep forgetting? If one day I look at your face and don't know who you are?"

She didn't want to think about that, but she knew where she would be if it came to pass. "I'll still be here. I promise."

It helped. A little. "You're a good girl, Carrie."

"I had a good teacher." She straightened, hooking her arm through his and drawing him toward her car. "Now come on, I'll take you home."

He looked at his own sedan. "What about the car?"

She opened the passenger side of her car. Her father looked too tired to drive home by himself, even if he was following her. "Don't worry, nobody'll take it. We'll come back for it in the morning, when you're feeling better. Now come on, Mom's fixing you some hot chocolate and amaretto."

"My favorite." He got in, then looked up at Caroline. "See, I remembered."

But his smile was sad.

Caroline called Dr. Wiseman at home early the next morning. Her father's appointment to review the tests was scheduled for close to noon, but she wanted to see the doctor as soon as he came into his office. Without her father. If the results were bad, she wanted time to find a way to break the news.

Because he was their friend, as well as their doctor, Wiseman came in early, opening the office himself. He led her to the back office, and then she sat, silent, while he reviewed the reports that a hospital courier had dropped off at five that morning.

And then he told her.

She took the news like a soldier. She had no choice. There was no one else there to share it with her. No one else in her life to share it with. Somehow, in the past few days, she had become the designated caretaker for both her parents.

The doctor's voice died away. Caroline sat numbly, staring at his Norman Rockwell print, on the wall behind him, where it had hung for the past thirty years. She had one just like it in her own cubbyhole at the clinic.

Strange, what stray thoughts wandered through your head at a time like this.

Caroline roused herself. "There's no mistake?"

"None. Caroline, this is *good* news. Your father doesn't have Alzheimer's."

No, but he had something else. Something that could potentially be just as devastating. And quicker to kill. "I never thought of a brain lesion as being good news."

He knew what she had to be feeling. He'd been a doctor too long not to. But she had to see the positive side.

"Operable ones are," he said firmly. "But we have to hurry." He flipped through his Rolodex, looked for a card he remembered inserting recently. "Right now, your father's walking around with a potential time bomb." He located the card and pulled it out. "Here." He handed it to her. "Alex Shaffer. He's been with the hospital just since January, but he's got a tremendous reputation. A merited reputation," Wiseman said emphatically. "Your father couldn't be better off than going to him for the surgery."

"Yes, he could," she said flatly. "He could not have this in the first place." And then she flushed. Wiseman was just trying to help. "I'm sorry, you're doing the best you can. I'm just a little shell-shocked, that's all. You never expect to hear this kind of thing yourself. It happens to other people." A rueful smile passed her lips. "I guess, to someone else, my father is 'other people.'" She pulled herself together. If she gave in and fell apart, her parents were sure to crumble. "How soon do you think we can get to see Shaffer?"

Leaning over the desk, Wiseman took the card back.

"Let me see what I can do." He was already tapping out the numbers on his keypad.

It was done. With lightning speed, things fell into place. By the end of the afternoon, arrangements had been made and her father admitted for a battery of preop tests and a workup. Surgery was scheduled for seven-thirty the following morning. There was no time to waste.

Caroline had handled it all, moving quickly, trying to stay one jump ahead of her thoughts. She refused to think until it was all over with. Refuse to admit, even to herself, that something could go wrong. It was hard enough dealing with the sight of her father, always such a powerful man, looking like an overgrown, lost boy in his hospital bed.

A hospital identification bracelet hanging from his wrist, he held her hand between his two large ones. His fingers felt cold.

"It's happening so fast, Carrie."

Was she rushing it? Was she hurrying away the last minutes her father might have? Caroline couldn't let the thought in. Instead, she gave him a bright, encouraging smile, the same one she'd worn for Joey when he looked at her, so frightened, as she applied the cast to his wrist.

"That's so you don't have time to worry. By this time next week, all this'll feel like a thing in the distant past. Better than that, you'll start being your old self again." She winked at him, ignoring the heart that was wrenching within her chest. "You might even remember where you left your reading glasses."

Because she could tease him, he felt heartened. "A man's got to have some kind of flaws."

"Not you, Joshua." Wanda did her best to choke back tears. "You were always perfect."

"Hey," he said, pretending to frown, "don't talk about me in the past tense. I'm right here. And I'm staying right here." His smile wavered as he looked at Caroline. "Right, Carrie?"

His voice was playful, but she knew he was asking for her assurance. She gave it freely. It was all she had to give.

"Right. You're not going anywhere, Dad." She glanced toward the door and saw a technician entering with a tray of vials and bottles. "But we are." Gently she moved her mother out of the way. "You are about to give this nice gentleman some blood."

"More blood?" Joshua winced. "Why can't they use some of the blood I gave on Friday?"

"They used it all up on other tests, remember?" She smiled and kissed him on the forehead. "Now don't argue and embarrass me. Remember, I have to work here. Behave yourself, you hear?"

The game faded. Joshua caught his daughter's hand again. He looked at her, a man uncertain about his future, about whether he had any future left at all after tomorrow at seven-thirty. "You'll be here in the morning?"

It broke her heart. "Right here, I promise. I'll be here to wish you luck. Don't worry, they won't start without me." She gently ushered her mother from the room. Behind them, the technician sat down beside her father and briskly began going about the business of blood-typing.

Her mother blew her father a kiss before the door closed.

The doorbell rang three times before she finally got to it. Her mother was in the family room with a few of her friends, women Caroline had called to come and take her mother's mind off tomorrow's surgery. She wasn't expecting anyone else.

Least of all the man in her doorway. "Sloan?"

She looked tired, he thought, and surprised to see him. Had he gotten his days mixed up? "Did I misunderstand? Weren't we supposed to go out to dinner tonight?"

He'd left his mother with the boys. She had won more in Vegas than she lost; her upbeat mood promised the boys a rare evening. It had helped make up for the disappointment when he told them that he wasn't bringing Caroline back to see them.

From the expression on her face, it looked as if he weren't bringing Caroline anywhere tonight.

"Oh, no, dinner." She'd completely forgotten. For a moment, she was torn. Her mother's need for diversion, for comfort, warred with her own. Maybe one of her friends could stay a while longer, while she—

No, it wasn't the same. And her mother needed her tonight. "I'm really sorry, Sloan, but I can't go. Something's come up."

He looked at the deep frown line furrowing her brow. "Something wrong?"

She didn't want to go into it. If she began, she wasn't sure she could stop. "No, I, um—"

He wasn't going to be pushed away. He knew all about pushing people away, and the consequences that came with it. Sloan didn't want that empty feeling for Caroline. Not when he saw how she was hurting.

"Caroline, something *is* wrong. Something's been wrong ever since you came back. Now, are we friends or aren't we?"

Her eyes met his. "We are."

The hand that gently touched her cheek offered nothing but comfort. "Friends are supposed to talk, remember?"

Caroline hesitated, silently debating with herself. Then she stepped out onto the porch, easing the door shut behind her. "Some of my mother's friends are inside. I called them so they could be with her for a while."

He tried to read between the lines. "Where's your dad?"

She took a deep breath. "In the hospital."

A car accident. The thought jumped up in huge capital letters. He struggled to keep the brutal memories in check. "Tell me."

The simple entreaty opened the floodgates. She could feel tears forming, and she lifted her head, as if gravity could keep them back. "I took him in early this afternoon. He's having surgery in the morning."

Sloan slipped his hand into hers. "Want to start at the beginning?"

No, she didn't want to start at the beginning. She wanted it all to be over with. She wanted life back the way it had been.

Caroline looked at Sloan and wet her lips. "I came home because my mother called me one night. She was almost crying, and she was very afraid. She said my father was acting strangely, forgetting things, having mood swings, things like that. Things that pointed to Alzheimer's disease."

"Oh, Caroline, I'm so sorry." He didn't know what to say. He only knew she shouldn't have to bear this sort of pain by herself. "Why didn't you tell me?"

She shrugged. "Because he wouldn't have wanted anyone to know. He wouldn't even admit the possibility to himself. I bullied him into going in for tests."

"I didn't know there was a test for Alzheimer's."

"There isn't." She thought of the rocky road others had to follow, and her heart went out to them. But the one her father was on might not be any better. "That's the diagnosis you arrive at by a process of elimination."

"And does he have it?"

Caroline looked up. There were stars in the sky, so many that it looked like a painting. How many times had she dreamed about standing under just such a sky with Sloan? It seemed ironic, somehow, that she'd finally gotten her wish at a time that was all wrong.

"No. He has a lesion on his brain. One that's growing rapidly." She recited the words the neurosurgeon had said. "It's pressing on the frontal lobe, and the surgeon's afraid it's going to embed itself where it'll become inoperable. We have to act fast.

"'We,'" she repeated, mocking herself. She sighed helplessly. "I have nothing to do with it. I can only stand by on the sidelines and say, 'Sure, Dad, have the surgery, it'll be all right.' 'Don't worry, Mom, Dad'll be just fine. Everything's just fine.'" She looked up at Sloan, feeling like such a hypocrite. "But it's not just fine. He could die, Sloan. My father could die, and the last thing he's going to remember is that I told him it was going to be 'just fine.'" Her throat grew dry. "That I lied to him."

She was torturing herself needlessly. Didn't she see that what she was doing was for everyone's good? That she was being unselfish? She had always been unselfish, he thought, remembering how she had tried to comfort him when, he knew, she was grieving herself. And he had pushed her away, because his wounds were too deep.

He wasn't going to let her push him away. "You're not lying. You're trying to make him feel better about what he has to face."

"That's me, little Miss Perky." Chilled to her very soul, she ran her hands up and down along her arms. "You know the worst of it? I can't cry. I mean, I can cry, but I can't. Not in front of them. My mother is hanging on to me, and my dad—my big, strong dad, who could face anything—he wants me to lie to him. He wants me to tell him it'll be all right. If I cry, if I cave in, they'll know that I'm as scared as they are. I can't show them that I'm scared. I don't have that luxury. But I am," she whispered. "Oh, Sloan, I am so scared."

She blinked back the tears she couldn't shed in front of anyone, turning her eyes up to Sloan. "I'm so tired of being brave, of pointing out the way when I don't know it myself. I'm so very tired." She dropped her head back, tears choking her throat. "What do I do?"

"You lean on me, Caroline," he told her, slipping an arm around her shoulders. He knew what it was like to face things alone, to put up a stone wall against the world and dare it to break through. He didn't want that for Caroline. "You can cry and lean on me."

Turning her around, he took her into his arms and just held her.

Caroline dropped her head down against his chest. The sound of her muffled sobs soaked into his shirt.

He held her tighter.

Chapter 9

"I don't think I can stand this, Caroline," Wanda whispered brokenly, her eyes fixed on the doors to the corridor as they closed. She held on to Caroline's arm for support.

Caroline placed her hand over her mother's. Beyond the electronic doors were the operating rooms. They had ridden down the elevator with her father and then walked alongside him to the doors as a wiry orderly silently pushed the gurney. The neurosurgeon had accompanied them, a blue cap covering his prematurely receding hairline, his body wrapped in hospital livery. His expression had been grave.

Crisply telling them that he would be out to see them once the surgery was over, he'd led the way in, leaving them on the other side of the doors. Wiseman had warned her that Shaffer's bedside manner left a great deal to be desired.

"But you don't want him because he's a good conversationalist, you want him because he's a damn good surgeon," he'd told her. Wiseman was right. She could do without the verbal reassurances, as long as she knew that she had someone who was exceptionally skilled fighting to save her father's life.

She felt her mother sway beside her, her face paling considerably. Wanda clutched at her hand like someone who was drowning.

"I don't think I can stand this, Caroline," she repeated, as if she hadn't just said the same words less than a minute ago.

Caroline couldn't stand by as she fell to pieces like this. But just giving her mother support wasn't going to be enough. It was time Wanda dug for some strength of her own.

Turning, Caroline faced her mother squarely. Using kid gloves hadn't worked. Maybe a little "tough love" would.

"Okay, now, you listen to me, Mother. You *can* stand it." Wanda began to shake her head in mute, tearful denial. Caroline steeled herself, refusing to be dissuaded. "You can stand a lot more than you think. Dad needs you now. He needs you to be there for him, the way you said you'd be. You can't just fall apart. It's not fair to him."

Tears gathered in the clear blue eyes, shimmering, threatening to spill out.

"But if he doesn't...if he doesn't..." Her soft voice broke, as she couldn't get herself to say the awful words.

Caroline stared into her mother's eyes, searching for some sign of strength to build on. It had to be there, some small, minuscule scrap she could work with.

"He will. He'll pull through. He's got an excellent surgeon and he's getting the best of care. Dad's a fighter, and he is going to pull through. You've got to believe that. Focus on it, do you hear me?'' Caroline ordered firmly. Her mother wasn't thinking anything that hadn't crossed her own mind a hundred times since yesterday morning, but dwelling on it would only paralyze both of them.

Numbed, Wanda nodded. ''All right,'' she said hoarsely. ''I believe it.''

She didn't, Caroline thought, but saying it was a start.

She looked around the hall. Great effort had been made to make the hospital look like a cheery place, where people came to be made well, rather than to die, but her mother needed to be out of here. Somewhere where dreaded possibilities weren't jumping out at her from around every corner.

Caroline slipped her arm around her mother's shoulders. Gently she guided her down the hall and away from the electronic doors.

''This is going to be a long procedure,'' she reminded her. ''It could take anywhere from four to six hours. I can call a cab for you, if you want. I'll tell the driver to take you to Frieda's house.'' She knew she could rely on her mother's best friend to keep her occupied for the duration of the surgery. She'd already broached the subject to Frieda, last night, before the woman left.

Wanda tried her best to concentrate on what Caroline was saying, but, filled with fear, her mind kept wandering. ''A cab? Where are you going to be?''

''Right here, Mom.'' Caroline had already made up her mind to remain. There was no way she was going to leave until she knew the outcome of the surgery, one way or another. ''I'll call you when he's in the recovery room. There's no use in both of us staying.'' They walked past the gift shop to a bank of telephones.

"Waiting here will only drive you up a wall. Dad wouldn't want that."

"Recovery room," Wanda echoed. "It has such a nice sound." If he was there, it would mean that Joshua was recovering, getting better. Becoming whole again, the way he used to be.

Caroline squeezed her mother's icy hand. "Yes, it does."

She waited with her mother at the front of the hospital until the cab arrived, some twenty minutes later. A light drizzle had started. Somehow, that seemed appropriate. Seeing her safely in and giving the driver the address, Caroline pressed forty dollars into her mother's hand for the fare and a tip. If she knew her mother, she wasn't carrying any money with her, other than spare change.

With a sense of minor relief, Caroline stood back and watched the cab drive away, then went inside again. The hours stretched before her as she walked to the area set aside for the friends and families of patients undergoing major surgery.

When the large, open room was remodeled in the last renovation wave, it had been decorated with an eye to comfort. Gone were the hard, uncomfortable orange plastic chairs. In their place were three long leather-upholstered sofas, arranged around a wide coffee table. The table was littered with magazines whose pages had been thumbed through but, for the most part, not seen.

A comfortable torture chamber, she thought as she approached it.

Caroline glanced at the graceful, bold-faced clock that hung over a fake fireplace. It would be hours before the craniotomy was over. Hours before she knew. Resigned, she settled in to wait, grateful that the room was empty at this hour. She wasn't up to making pleasant, banal conversation with complete strangers.

"I wondered where you had gotten to."

Caroline jerked, turning to look behind her. Her heart skipped a beat, then came down hard in double time. She thought she was imagining things. But he was still standing there. Like the answer to an unspoken prayer.

"Sloan. What are you doing here?"

"Looking for you." He sat down beside her on the sofa. The leather sighed softly, accepting the new weight. "I wandered all over the first floor before I took a ride up to your father's room. They said he'd been taken to surgery, so I knew I didn't get the time mixed up."

She was staring at him like some tongue-tied idiot, and she still didn't understand what he was doing here.

"But why—?" This was Tuesday, right? "Aren't you supposed to be in school?"

"I graduated." His smile was quick, warming as he winked at her. He had been right, Sloan thought as he studied her face. She needed company. "I took a personal day."

Her mind just didn't seem to be functioning. "Why?"

Did she really have to ask? "Simple. Because I don't think you should be alone at a time like this. I came to hold your hand."

She wasn't fit company right now. It was bad enough that she had broken down in front of him last night. "You've got things to do. The boys, the play, your classes..." Her voice trailed off as she ran out of things to enumerate.

She could push him away all she wanted, but he wasn't leaving. Patiently Sloan refuted her objections, one by one.

"I already told you, I took a personal day. The play isn't for another two weeks, and rehearsal's at four. The boys are in school. My mother's going to pick them up if I can't make it." Satisfied that he had covered everything, he told her, "And I don't have anything to do that's more important than being here with you right now." As he looked into her eyes, Sloan knew he hadn't said anything truer in a long time. It surprised him a little.

He saw the stress, even though she hid it well. "How are you holding up?"

"Great, fine." The protest rang hollow even to her own ears. She flashed a quirky smile, mocking herself. "Do you mind if I squeeze the fingers off your hand?"

He held it out to her. "Squeeze away, if it helps."

"No, what helps is having you here. I know how you feel about hospitals. Thank you." The words felt hopelessly inadequate.

Since she didn't take his hand, he took hers. Her fingers were like ice, even though the room was pleasantly warm. Sloan enveloped them with his other hand. "Hey, what are friends for?"

"Mom?" Caroline covered her other ear with her hand to block out the noise coming from the gift shop, directly behind her.

"Caroline?" Her mother uttered her name breathlessly, fear weaving through every syllable. "What's happened? Should I come down? Oh, God," she said on a sob, "he's gone, isn't he?"

Caroline knew she should have told Frieda it was all right before she put her mother on the phone, but she had been too excited about giving her the news to think logically.

"No, Mom, he's not gone. Dad came through. The operation's over, and he came through." The tears of relief were still clinging to her lashes. She blinked them away. "Dr. Shaffer said they got it all. Dad's going to be all right."

After finally allowing herself to think the worst, Wanda was almost afraid to believe the good news. "No more forgetting?"

Caroline laughed. Her father had always had a tendency to forget birthdays and anniversaries. "No more than usual."

As she spoke, she glanced behind her. Sloan was standing by the gift shop to give her a little privacy. Looking in her direction, he smiled. If she hadn't already been in love with him, she would have fallen in love with him today. He'd been so kind, so considerate, making her laugh when she would have sworn that wasn't possible. She hadn't been wrong when she fell for him all those years ago. He was a good man.

"Mom, why don't you stay with Frieda for a while longer? I just want to hang around until they bring Dad back up to his room."

Wanda hesitated, undecided. "Should I come down, too? He'll want to know why I'm not there."

"No, stay with Frieda." It would be better for everyone concerned if her mother saw her father when he was awake. "The doctor said Dad's going to be out of it pretty much the rest of the day."

A glimmer of fear returned. "You're not keeping anything from me, are you?"

No, not this time, Mom. "No, I'm not. I'm just looking out for you, Mom." *The way I always have.* She debated saying something further, then decided there was no harm in it. "Sloan came down to keep me company. I thought I'd—"

About some things, Wanda was intuitive. "I always liked that boy."

A smile played across Caroline's lips as she looked at him. At thirty-two, Sloan was hardly a boy. "You've got good taste, Mom. I'll see you later."

"I love you, Caroline."

The declaration took her by surprise. She wasn't accustomed to her mother saying that to her. But then, today had been far from an ordinary day. "I love you too, Mom." Caroline hung up.

As soon as she did, Sloan joined her. "Everything okay?"

She nodded. "Yes. My mother said she always liked you," she added whimsically.

A smile played on his lips. "Smart lady, your mother." Sloan was glad to see the stress gone from her eyes. So easily that it seemed as if he'd been doing it forever, he slipped his arm around her shoulders and guided her away from the phones. "So, you want to go somewhere and celebrate?"

She was already drunk with relief and euphoria. Celebrating seemed almost anticlimactic. Caroline looked up at him, suddenly very aware of his proximity. Now that the worst had passed, she could allow herself to dwell on the fact that Sloan had cared enough to put himself out for her.

"Sure." She veered away from the course he had set toward the front doors, leading him instead to the elevators located at the rear of the hospital. "I hear the cafeteria makes a mean ham and cheese sandwich."

He groaned as they passed the gift shop again. Stuffed animals in various bright colors, and one discreetly tasteful negligee, decorated the single small window. "Oh, please, cafeteria food?"

She'd already sampled it during her shifts, and she could honestly recommend it.

"You'd be surprised. This is an outstanding hospital in more ways than one." When he seemed to resist, she linked her arm through his. "Come on, it doesn't matter where we go, it's the company. Besides, I know what a teacher's salary is like. Even an outstanding teacher like you."

There were never any pretenses with Caroline, he thought. And she was right. It wasn't the food, it was the company. He liked being with her, felt better being with her, even when he was the one offering her moral support.

"All right, cafeteria food it is. If we need our stomachs pumped, at least we're in the right place." They stopped by the elevators, and Caroline pressed the down button. His eyes skimmed over her face. "You know you're positively radiant, don't you?"

"I get that way when I'm happy, and right now," she said, her eyes holding his, "I'm on top of the world." She paused, looking for the right words. How did you thank someone for keeping you from falling apart? "I don't know what I would have done without you."

"You'd have managed. You always do, Caroline." The elevator doors opened. They waited until it emptied out, then got on. They had the car to themselves. Sloan reached over and pressed for the basement. "You might look like a cream puff, but you're the strongest person I know."

Caroline arched an eyebrow. "Cream puff?"

"Cream puff." He looked her over, taking her measure. "You're what, about five-one and maybe a hundred and five pounds? That qualifies as a cream puff in my book.''

She lifted her chin. "That's five-one-and-a-quarter and a hundred pounds, thank you very much.''

Sloan laughed. "Big difference, that quarter of an inch.''

Caroline raised herself up on her toes to emphasize the point, feeling positively giddy. "Yes, it is.'' She nodded smartly. "And don't you forget it.''

It happened quickly, maybe even without his knowledge. His instincts suddenly just took over. When she stood on her toes, Caroline's mouth was tantalizingly close to his. Even closer, if he inclined his head.

He did, softly touching his lips to hers. He wasn't sure just what had come over him. Maybe he had gotten caught up in her happiness. Maybe he just wanted to tap into it. He didn't know. All he knew was that one moment he was sharing her laughter, the next moment he was sharing the overwhelmingly sweet taste of her mouth.

Sharing it, and losing a bit of himself in the bargain. Kissing her was getting to be a habit. A very addicting habit. She tasted of cherries. Sloan had always had a weakness for cherries.

Caroline's surprise gave way to pleasure, and then something far more powerful, that curled like smoke within her. Caroline stretched up against him, wrapping her arms around Sloan's neck, her soul around his mouth.

"Fraternizing with the clientele?''

Caroline drew quickly away from Sloan, trying to orient herself. Kissing him had managed to transport her to a totally other place in time and space. A vacuum where only the two of them existed.

A place without elevator doors that opened at inopportune times.

Dr. Wiseman walked into the elevator, an amused smile lifting the ends of his graying mustache. "I came down for a cup of coffee to celebrate. Alex Shaffer just had me paged to tell me that your father's surgery went well." His eyes washed over her, then Sloan. "I guess we all have our own ways of celebrating."

The doors began to close again. Coming to life, Caroline quickly pressed the open button. "Dr. Wiseman, this is Sloan Masters, a...friend."

"Glad to meet you, Sloan Masters, a friend." Sloan acknowledged the greeting with a nod of his head as he followed Caroline out of the elevator.

"I'd tell you to take good care of her, but I see that you already are." Wiseman smiled at them knowingly. "Oh, Caroline." He stuck his hand between the doors just as they began to close. They sprang open again. "Don't bother coming in tonight. I took the liberty of talking to Paulette and told her your father was having surgery this morning. She sends her good wishes. You have the evening off."

Paulette was the woman who coordinated the different shifts in the emergency room. It seemed Wiseman knew everyone. "Thank you, but you didn't have to put yourself out like that."

Orchestrating conveniences was no trouble at all. He enjoyed it. "Hey, I'm a G.P.," he reminded her. "I have to try harder." The doors began to close again. "I'll be by to look in on your dad later," Wiseman promised. "Unofficially."

"Nice guy," Sloan commented as they started walking down the corridor to the cafeteria.

"The best." She looked up at him. The smile she

offered worked its way straight into his gut. It had a lot in common with her kiss, he thought. Same kind of punch. Almost. "There's a lot of that going around lately."

"Are you sure you don't mind?" Sloan asked again, getting out of his car. He'd brought her with him, but he was still dubious about it. "After all, this is your evening off." Now that the crisis had passed, maybe she wanted some time to herself.

Yes, it was her evening off, Caroline thought, and she was spending it just the way she wanted to. She got out, smoothing her skirt. She waited until he rounded the hood and joined her before walking toward the front steps that led to the school.

"My father's resting comfortably. My mother is spending the night with her oldest friend, and the way I see it, I owe *my* oldest friend a favor. You said you wanted an impartial eye to see how your play is coming along, and I'm as impartial as they get."

He pulled open the door and held it for her. "We're keeping tally of favors now?"

"No." She grinned at him. "As long as I don't owe one."

She'd never felt comfortable being on the receiving end of a kindness or a favor without turning around and giving something back in return. When Sloan mentioned his concern about being an impartial judge of his students' efforts, she'd seen her chance to pay him back in a minor way.

Sloan knew better than to argue. "You have your own way of thinking, you know that?"

She grinned. "So they tell me." Caroline looked

around. Everything seemed so familiar. Nostalgia flooded her. "Hasn't changed much, has it?"

"No. The lockers still stick. Mr. Hackett's gut still hangs out over his belt by a mile," he said, referring to his old P.E. teacher, "although he's gotten a little grayer."

"Does Mr. Cleary still wear that awful toupee?"

"No, that's changed," he realized. "He's gone natural. His wife's told him that bald is sexy. It might be," Sloan was willing to concede. "But not in Cleary's case." He pushed open one of the two black padded doors that led into the auditorium. "Okay, don't say I didn't try to talk you out of this."

"I promise I won't sue you if I fall asleep," she said teasingly.

Allison turned at the sound of the auditorium door opening. She'd been here over an hour, waiting for Sloan to arrive. Hoping he'd come early, so that they could finally be alone together. That plan had been dashed when students began trickling in a few minutes ago. Still, she was happy he was finally here.

The quickening of her heart dulled when she saw that he wasn't alone.

"Looks like you've got competition," her best friend, Dorothy, whispered in her ear.

Allison tossed her head, annoyed at the implication. "A lot you know." But her confidence was shaken.

Putting on her most seductive smile, she glided up the aisle. With the moves of an agile cat, Allison maneuvered herself between Sloan and the woman he'd brought with him.

"Mr. Walters, you brought your sister to watch our play? We're not nearly ready yet."

Sloan moved ahead of the girl, thinking it was safer that way. "You're underestimating yourself." He tossed the words over his shoulder. "And this isn't my sister. This is Dr. Masters. She's kindly agreed to preview our play."

His attention directed toward the students onstage, Sloan dropped his briefcase on a seat in the first row. He missed the look in Allison's eyes.

But Caroline didn't.

She recognized it instantly. Years ago, she'd seen the very same look in her own reflection. She would have been less than human not to feel a little sorry for the girl. "You're Allison, aren't you?"

Allison slanted a suspicious look in Caroline's direction. "Yes, I am. How did you know?"

"Mr. Walters told me all about you."

The suspicious look deepened, until it furrowed along her brow.

"How good you were in the play," Caroline explained. "He thinks you have natural talent."

Allison chewed on her lower lip, wishing she could show Sloan just how naturally talented she was. Still, a compliment was a compliment. "He did?"

"Absolutely. And that he was relying on you to help Matt along." She took the seat next to the one with Sloan's briefcase. "How's that going?"

Allison wasn't entirely sure how to react to the open display of friendliness. "Oh, okay, I guess."

Sloan *had* told her that Allison was good. And that he thought Matt Prescott would do anything to live up to Allison's expectations of him. "You're just being modest, aren't you?"

Flustered, confused, Allison shook her head. "No, not really. I—"

"Places, people," Sloan called out. He looked over his shoulder. "You, too, Allison. We're taking the whole play from the top."

"But I don't know all my lines," a strawberry blonde in front protested.

"Do the best you can. This isn't a final rehearsal. I just want to get a feel for the whole performance, see where we still need work. Nobody's going to take you out behind the barn and shoot you if you forget your lines." He grinned at them. "Not yet, anyway." He looked at the nine-piece orchestra. "We'll begin with the overture."

Caroline settled back to be entertained.

Chapter 10

Sloan waited until all the students had left the auditorium. They had gone through an entire run-through of the play, and then he'd outlined for them what still needed work. Occasionally he'd turned toward Caroline to gauge her reaction when a particular bit of business worked in the production. Each time, it had looked as if she were delighted. She had certainly laughed in all the right places. The students had eaten it up and given it their all.

But he knew Caroline. She might have just been being kind. One way or another, he wanted to know her honest gut reaction.

"So, what do you think?"

Did he realize that, blasé though he tried to be, he was wearing his heart on his sleeve? This play was very important to him. That was what she had always loved about him. He cared about things, about people's feelings.

She was relieved that she didn't have to lie to spare him. "I think you have hidden talents."

Her answer bewildered him. "I mean about the play."

"I'm talking about the play." She followed him up the aisle to the rear doors. "You've managed to find the right person for each role. A little more polish, and this little high school play of yours could be mistaken for a professional production." He looked so relieved, she could have hugged him. "But you already knew that."

"No, I hoped that. There's a difference." He held the outer door open for her. "Sometimes you're just too close to something to know."

Amen to that, Caroline thought.

The front parking lot had almost cleared out. One parent, driving a light green van, was picking up three girls at the end of the curb. Caroline saw Allison standing on the steps. The teenager who played Frank Butler was talking to her, but the girl's attention was obviously aimed in their direction. In Sloan's direction, Caroline amended.

"Know what else I think?" She got into the passenger seat, waiting for Sloan to come around to the driver's side.

Was there more? "No, what?" Sloan pulled the seat belt taut, inserting the metal tongue in the slot.

She nodded discreetly toward Allison as they drove out of the lot. "I think that girl has a serious crush on you."

He frowned. It wasn't something he wanted to hear. He was hoping that he'd been mistaken in his assessment, that it had just been his imagination. "You think so?"

There was no guesswork about it. "I know so," she answered with finality.

The light ahead began turning red. Sloan sighed, easing his foot onto the brake. ''Maybe I should have a talk with her.''

Caroline looked at him, stunned. Was he crazy? No, he wasn't crazy, he was kind, and he probably thought he could handle this if he was just gentle enough. Gorgeous hunk of manhood or not, Sloan Walters had a lot to learn about women.

''And say what?'' she wanted to know. ''That you're very flattered? That if she were ten years older and not your student, things might be different?''

He assumed, from her tone, that that wasn't the way to go. ''Not in those exact words, but yes, more or less.''

''Very bad move.''

''Why?'' It seemed only logical to him.

Caroline settled back against the seat as the light turned green again. ''Well, in less than a couple of months, she won't be your student anymore, she'll be a high school graduate. And as for the age thing, she'll tell you it doesn't matter to her. And you, sir, will be in big trouble. My advice to you is just to ignore it as long as you can. Be yourself.'' A smile played across her lips as she glanced at him. ''Be oblivious to it.''

Sloan jockeyed for position with a meat truck. The truck won. Sloan drove around it. ''Are you saying I don't notice things?''

Her laugh answered him before she did. ''You are the type who wouldn't notice your nose if you were looking into a mirror, unless you were specifically searching for it.'' And she was living proof of that. She'd known him before Julie did. Loved him before Julie did. But he'd never taken notice of that. He hadn't known love until it flamboyantly sizzled before him, with flowing black hair and bright green eyes framed with the longest, blackest lashes God ever created.

"Thanks a lot." He snorted. They sped through the next intersection, making it before the light had a chance to turn red. "And since when did you get to be such an expert on crushes?"

She should have anticipated the question. Caroline faced forward, keeping her tone light. "I had one myself once."

A stolen glance told Caroline that he'd turned to look at her, one eyebrow raised in surprised curiosity. He probably thought he knew all about her. Which just showed how little he did know. "Who?"

She shrugged the question away carelessly. "That's unimportant."

"Not to me." Sloan paused, going over in his mind all the male teachers who had been at Bedford High while they were students. He couldn't come up with any likely candidates. "Come on, Caroline, give. What teacher sent your pulse racing?" When she said nothing, he purposely selected the one who wouldn't have been anyone's choice. "Mr. Hackett?"

"Oh, please." Caroline rolled her eyes. It had always remained a mystery to her how the man could ever have found someone to marry him. But then, she reminded herself, she had never met Mrs. Hackett. Mr. Hackett might have turned out to be the better bargain of the two. "And besides, it wasn't a teacher."

Now why the hell had she volunteered that? She'd be better off if he went on thinking that she was exactly like Allison.

Sloan turned on the corner, guiding the car down his street. "Oh, unrequited love. This is getting even better."

"Not really." There were questions forming and multiplying in his mind; she could almost see them coming together. With relief, she pointed toward his house. "We've arrived."

And none too soon, I might add.

Sloan didn't see that as a reason to bring an end to the conversation. "C'mon, Caroline, tell me. Who was it?" He got out of the car and waited for her to join him. "We're supposed to be friends."

"And if we're going to remain friends, you're going to have to stop pestering me." She jerked a thumb toward the beveled front door. "Now open the door and let me greet my fan club."

He sifted through his key ring, looking for his house key. Emotionally, Caroline had put in a long day. She'd be better off going home and getting some rest. "Sure you're up to this? I can still take you home."

"What, walk away from two short men who want to throw their arms around me and tell me that they've missed me?" She took the keys from his hand and inserted the right one in the lock. "Not a chance. I know what you're up to. You just want to hog them all to yourself."

Most people were overwhelmed by his twosome. Even his mother had trouble lasting more than a day, and she had them more or less trained. That Caroline was looking forward to seeing them touched Sloan in places he usually kept tucked away from the world.

He placed his hand over Caroline's as she started to turn the doorknob. She raised her eyes to his questioningly. "You're pretty amazing, you know that?"

"So you keep telling me."

And someday, if she was very, very lucky, he was going to mean that just the way she wanted him to, not because she had uncommon endurance when it came to kids or because she could remain calm in a crisis or even because she'd grown a backbone at the age of eighteen. He was going to say it because he saw her for the woman she was and loved her for it.

Dream on.

Just then, the door flew open, pulled from within. Joey edged Danny out with his cast and was the first to attach himself to her waist. He was completely oblivious to the fact that he had smacked her with his cast. "Yow're here."

Caroline cocked her head, listening. "And you're lisping." She cupped his chin in her hand and tilted it up to survey his mouth. Her suspicions were confirmed. "You lost a tooth, Joey."

Joey shook his head as he dug into his front pocket. "No, I didn't. It's wight here." He proudly held it up for her to see. He'd washed it off himself.

Disgusted, Danny scowled at his brother. "He's got all the luck."

Attracted by the commotion, Joan Masters walked in to join them. "Joey and his cast were the center of attention in the schoolyard today," she explained. She ruffled her other grandson's hair fondly. "Danny's feeling a little left out." She smiled a greeting at the woman her son had brought in. The smile was identical to the one that winked across Sloan's lips. Beyond that, the family resemblance was all but nonexistent. "Hello, Caroline. How's your father?"

She appreciated the inquiry. "Terrific," Caroline told her. "The doctor said he's going to be just fine." It felt good to say those words and actually mean them for a change. "And as for you, young man..." Eyeing Danny, she threw one arm around his shoulders and pulled him to her. "Don't you know you can never be left out? Big brothers are always really important guys. Look how you looked out for Joey after the accident. Think that doesn't rack up points?"

Danny considered her question. He didn't have a clue. "With who?"

She looked at Sloan before answering. "With all the people who count." Putting out her other hand, she drew Joey closer to her. "C'mon, guys, let's go see what we can find in the refrigerator for your dad. He's been a real good Scout today."

Boy, how did Caroline know all this stuff? "I didn't know Dad was a Boy Scout," Danny said.

She grinned as she looked over her shoulder at Sloan. He'd certainly come through for her today. It had felt wonderful to have someone to turn to, someone's hand to hold. "Of major proportions."

Joey piped up. "What's that mean?"

She nodded toward the kitchen. "Come help me and I'll explain." She ushered them from the room.

"Hard to believe that's Caroline Masters," Joan commented as she slipped her arms into a sweater, preparing to leave. "I can remember when she was such a little mouse. I guess people do change."

Handing his mother her purse, Sloan followed her to the door. "I guess they do."

A typical vague comment, but that was a man for you. Even if he was her son. Probably didn't even have a clue that the woman was in love with him. Joan smiled to herself as she left.

Well, Sloan would see for himself in time. And if not, Joan silently promised, she'd help him. Sloan needed someone like Caroline in his life.

* * *

Caroline took another sip of the punch Sloan had handed her. From its kick, it was apparent that someone had decided that rum was an integral ingredient in punch. She remembered when someone had spiked the punch during one of the school dances. The principal had been livid, but the culprit or culprits had never been found. Their handiwork had tasted nearly as good as this.

"You're really going to do it?" Sloan asked.

She let the liquid slide down her throat before continuing.

"I guess it's going to go on record as one of the shortest tours of duty, so to speak, on record at Harris Memorial." She was referring to her work in the emergency room. "I'll still be on staff, of course." She set the glass down behind her on the buffet table. "But not in the ER. Not unless someone asks for me personally," she added.

After a little more than a week on the job, with one personal day taken for her father's surgery, Caroline had handed in her notice. She'd made up her mind about her future. At least part of it.

"Then you're staying in Bedford permanently?"

She nodded.

Sloan wondered whether the warmth he felt had something to do with her answer, or just with the second glass of punch he'd just drained. He had a sneaking suspicion is was more the former than the latter. That made him a little nervous, but he couldn't quite pinpoint why. "What made you change your mind?"

You, you idiot, among other things. She tried to maintain an impassive face as she answered. "My folks are getting older, and it's easier for me to be close by than to have to drop everything and travel across two states whenever something comes up."

Not that it looked as if there were going to be any family emergencies anytime soon. Her father was doing far better than the neurosurgeon had initially anticipated. Just maybe not as fast as her father would be satisfied with. But then, he'd always been demanding when it came to himself. And as her father grew stronger, so did her mother. Caroline had actually gotten her to balance the checkbook today. Yes, things on the home front were moving along splendidly.

It made her feel homesick, just thinking about going away again.

"Besides, coming back to Bedford reminded me how much I miss this place. It's growing so fast. I want to be here before I don't recognize it at all anymore."

Sloan couldn't remember when he'd been so pleased over a piece of news. "That's great."

If she let herself, she could get swept up in the enthusiasm in his voice. But she held fast, grounding herself. Disappointment was always harder to take if you fell from a higher perch.

Still, she couldn't help prodding just a little. "It is?"

"Sure, Danny and Joey will be thrilled. They've taken to you the way I have never seen them take to anyone before."

Danny and Joey would be thrilled. She already knew that. What she didn't know was how he felt about her remaining. She bit her lip to keep from blurting the question out. "Well, it's not exactly like I'm a stranger."

He had another point of view. "Up until now, you almost were. You've been back, what?" He tried to remember. "A handful of times since you went off to college?"

She shrugged, looking out on the dance floor. A band comprised of former students who'd once been in the orchestra was playing a medley of romantic songs. Mr. Hackett was taking a turn on the floor with Mrs. Jenkins, holding her as close as space permitted. Mrs. Jenkins was stoically bearing up to it. Mr. Hackett was having the time of his life. You'd have thought it was *his* retirement party.

"I never counted." *Ten,* she thought. *I've been back ten times, and once was for your wedding.* After that, the visits had grown fewer in number. Her parents had come up to see her on holidays and various other occasions, rather than the other way around. Caroline had preferred it that way.

He took her answer at face value. "Well, it was only a handful, and the boys never really got to know you, certainly not the way they have now. Even when you were here on visits, you were a lot shier then than you are now."

If you could notice that, why couldn't you notice that I was in love with you—before you fell for Julie?

It was a moot point. Water under the bridge, her mother liked to say. Sloan hadn't noticed then that she was in love with him, and he still didn't notice. When he kissed her, there was no way for him to realize that he made her blood rise and sent her head spinning so that she was completely disoriented. He wasn't the kind to notice things like that.

Why was she torturing herself, going over old ground like this?

It had to be the gym. There were memories here.

When she learned of the faculty's intention to throw her a party of their own, Mrs. Jenkins had told them in no uncertain terms that she wouldn't attend unless they held the party in the gymnasium. The gymnasium where she had sat in the bleachers, cheering for the Bedford

Panthers basketball team every home game they played. She'd been a fixture here. Like as not, she still would be once she retired. The school and its various interconnecting concerts, games and plays were her life.

Sloan wished there was a way to open a window. There were too many people crowded in here. That would account for the short supply of air. Why else would he have trouble drawing a complete breath without feeling just the slightest bit light-headed?

Or maybe it was Caroline's perfume that was to blame. Her perfume that reminded him of flowers on a hillside. Heavily scented flowers that clouded a man's mind and his senses so that he couldn't think straight.

The band was good. He'd always had trouble resisting music's allure, he thought. And it was so long since he'd actually danced.

Sloan turned toward Caroline, putting on his most persuasive expression. "So, do you want to take a turn around the floor?"

She looked at the various couples uncertainly. "As in dancing?"

What an odd question. "Unless you want to dribble a basketball on the court and shoot a few hoops."

At least she knew how to do that, thanks to the efforts of a college roommate whose brother played semipro ball. "I'd be better at that than dancing."

He raised an eyebrow in mock surprise. "What, suddenly shy Caroline again?" He took her hand, not waiting for her answer. "Come on, there's nothing to it." Facing her, he took her into his arms. "I'll lead."

Each time they were like this, it got to feel more and more as if this were where she belonged.

Illusion, nothing but illusion. "I was kind of hoping you'd do that."

His hand on the small of her back, he began to move in time with the music. He wasn't even aware of what his feet were doing. He was far more aware of what her body, pressed ever so lightly against him, was doing to him.

Sloan tucked her hand in his, resting it against his chest. "See, nothing to it."

Nothing except the warm glow she felt, her body swaying against his in time to a melody that wafted into her very soul.

Just as he did.

Was that his heart that was beating so hard? Or hers?

Probably hers, she thought. His heart would never beat so erratically because they were so close.

"No," she said quietly, looking up at him, "nothing to it at all."

Nothing was not the word to it.

Did she feel it? he wondered. This spark, this electricity, that seemed to appear every time he was this close to her? Or was that all just a figment of his imagination?

What had gotten into him, anyway? Kissing her, looking for excuses to hold her in his arms, that wasn't like him.

This was Caroline, for heaven's sake. He'd known her half of his life. Longer. She was his friend, she was…she was…

Beautiful, he thought. Wearing a simple blue-gray dress, the ends of her honey brown hair skimming her almost bare shoulders, and wearing some fragrance that insisted on filling every empty cavity in his head, Caroline was beautiful.

Why hadn't he ever noticed that?

You wouldn't notice your nose if you were looking in the mirror, unless you were specifically searching for it.

Her words replayed themselves in his head. Maybe she was right, he thought. Maybe he didn't see unless he was searching.

But he wasn't searching for anything now, Sloan insisted. He certainly wasn't searching for anyone to love, no matter how incomplete he felt. He'd had one perfect love in his life, and he was content with that.

Should be content with that.

He turned Caroline once around the floor as the tempo increased. It pleased him that she managed to keep up.

If he was content with his life, with the way things were, why was he having these thoughts? Why were these urges sneaking up on him, delivering one-two punches when he least expected it? Why did kissing her feel so exhilarating that he craved more each time?

If he was so content, why did he wonder what it would be like to lose himself in her, really lose himself? To bury his face in her hair, to slowly kiss every inch of her body and make love with her until this miserable ache went away?

There was such a strange look in his eyes. "What are you thinking?"

Her question broke up his mental reverie. Sloan cleared his throat before replying. It had gone as dry as dust. Did she see something in his eyes? No, she would have made a joke about it if she had. She wouldn't think of them as a couple, much less as lovers.

And neither should he.

He covered quickly. "I'm thinking what a fast learner you are."

Of course. Although, for just a tiny precious second, she'd thought...hoped...

She was being an idiot again. "One of my gifts," she quipped. She turned away as a shaft of sadness drove itself into her. "There's Mrs. Jenkins. Maybe we should say a word to the guest of honor?"

Before he could reply, Caroline grabbed his hand and led him off the dance floor. It was a matter of survival. She couldn't take any more. Having him so close to her was both heaven and hell. Heaven because he was there, and hell because she knew in her heart that she would never be anything more than a friend to him.

That should be enough, she upbraided herself.

The tingling sensation in her body told her there was another opinion on the matter.

Mrs. Jenkins had just sent Mr. Hackett off to his wife. Following the coach with her eyes, Caroline was surprised to discover that his wife was a very pretty, petite woman. She smiled to herself. Obviously, there was more to the man than she thought.

Very lightly, Caroline tapped Mrs. Jenkins on the shoulder. "Mrs. Jenkins, you probably don't remember me, but I'm—"

Mary Jenkins peered over the tops of her half glasses. "Caroline Masters. Third row, center. You've gotten prettier." She looked at the young man she'd once threatened to flunk. He'd turned out rather nicely, she mused, feeling as if at least a tiny bit of credit for that belonged to her. "Hasn't she, Sloan?"

Sloan smiled his agreement. "I was just thinking that."

His answer flustered her. Caroline had to concentrate on gathering her thoughts together. She focused on Mrs. Jenkins. The woman was nothing short of incredible. "I don't know whether to blush at the compliment or be astounded by your memory."

Mrs. Jenkins made a ruling on the choice. "Oh, be astounded, by all means. Blushing is a complete waste of time," she said, waving a dismissing hand at the thought, "unless you're doing it around a man that sort of thing charms." She slanted a look at Sloan before continuing.

Sloan was about to protest the assumption, but then he realized that maybe he did find that sort of thing charming. At least on Caroline.

The older woman cocked her head, looking very much like a bird studying a hole renowned for its ample supply of worms. Her eyes scrutinized Caroline.

"So, I hear you're a pediatrician now. Plenty of babies in Bedford." A look of sadness momentarily flickered over her face. "Plenty of babies I won't be able to teach." And then the look passed, as she trained her hawklike eyes on Caroline. "How about it?"

Had she missed something? "Excuse me?"

"I don't remember your attention span being deficient in class, Caroline. I thought I made my question perfectly clear. How about returning here to practice?"

It looked as if Caroline were about to be grilled. Sloan came to her rescue. "As a matter of fact, Caroline is talking about doing that."

The news pleased her. Mary nodded her gray head with as much enthusiasm as anyone had ever witnessed coming from her. "Splendid." Her gaze was meaningful as she turned it on Sloan. "Good for you."

Sloan held up his hands. "I can't take credit for that. I didn't have anything to do with it."

Mrs. Jenkins gave every indication that she thought otherwise. "As you wish." She turned her attention to Caroline one last time. "Tell me, did you ever come to terms with the fact that two parallel lines meet at infinity?''

She'd forgotten that had ever troubled her. Now she remembered—she'd had a terrible time with the concept. It had been one of the few times she was prompted to contest something a teacher said. ''No, but I'm working on it.''

Mrs. Jenkins nodded. ''That's all one can ask. That, and to make the most of the life that's given to you. It's very precious and very fleeting.''

Confused silence greeted her words.

Mary Jenkins looked thoughtfully at them, studying their faces, before she spoke. And then she made up her mind. ''Did you ever wonder why I spent so much time at school?''

Feeling a little awkward, Caroline exchanged looks with Sloan. ''I always thought it was because you liked the students.''

''Oh, of course, there's that, but a large part of it was because there was no one waiting for me at home. I lost my husband and my only child when I was very young.'' She didn't go into any details. Those belonged to her alone. ''Now, I didn't tell you to get your sympathy,'' she said, bristling at the look she saw in their eyes. ''Nothing I hate more than sympathy. I'm telling you so that someday you're not on the receiving end of sympathy. Or, worse, self-pity. Make the most of the life you're given,'' she repeated. ''And grab what's just out of reach.''

Satisfied that she had made her point, she squared her shoulders. ''Now, if you'll excuse me, I have to go and bore someone else.''

With that, she turned and walked away from them.

Chapter 11

Sloan had a far better time at the retirement party than he had anticipated. He and Caroline remained until almost the end, and were among the last three couples to leave.

A couple. It was strange, thinking of himself as part of a couple again, even if it was by mistake. That had been his initial reaction when someone referred to Caroline and him as a couple at the party.

Ed Hackett had called them that, just before he stole Caroline away, claiming her for one dance.

"Never thought I'd see the two of you as a couple. But I guess that's because, back then, you didn't look the way you do now." The P.E. teacher chuckled lasciviously at his own comment before taking her into his arms.

Caroline had handled him with ease. When had she become such an adroit social creature? Sloan wondered.

No one could have been more surprised than Sloan

when he caught himself watching her and being concerned when Hackett took her to the dance floor. A lot of things surprised Sloan about himself lately. Ever since Caroline had returned to Bedford.

As he drove away from the high school parking lot now, the coach's words replayed themselves in his mind. He and Caroline, a couple.

Denial came, but not as quickly as before. Not nearly as quickly as he would have thought it should.

Why?

Was it because, just for a little while, he'd enjoyed the sensation of being part of a couple? Of being half of a whole again? He'd been a solitary half for so long, and the ache to belong, to be healed, was no less now than it had been to begin with; he just didn't like to admit it, even to himself.

He sighed, turning on his turn signal. Yellow-white beams bounced off the car in front of him, highlighting an out-of-state license plate. Hawaii. Even people who lived in paradise wanted to go to other places, to see if there was anything better beyond their borders, he mused. Maybe there could be more than one paradise.

He slanted a look at Caroline and wondered.

She'd had a wonderful time, and she didn't want to see it end. Was this what Cinderella felt like, just before the clock struck midnight? Probably. But she was grateful for what she'd had.

She wanted more.

The curse of human nature, Caroline thought with a philosophical sigh. Never satisfied.

Silence had never bothered him when he was around Caroline. But just this once, it begged for music. Sloan flipped the radio on.

A high-pitched screech of static pierced the air before he could turn it down.

"Joey's been fiddling with the dial again," he muttered. One eye on the road, he searched for his favorite station. Finding it, he turned the volume up a little again. A steady, catchy beat began to undulate, seeping through the car. Through both of them. It was hard not to move and keep time.

It made him think of the song that had been playing when Mr. Hackett came over to them. Sloan laughed to himself.

"Is this a private joke, or can I hear it?"

He glanced at her, still laughing. They had looked so mismatched on the floor, she and Hackett. "I think watching you dance with Coach Hackett was worth the price of admission."

Caroline grinned, taking no offense. "I had no idea my arms could stretch that far." All things considered, she was rather fond of the high school coach. From her perspective as a physician, she saw reason to be concerned about his health. "You know, he's not exactly a shining example of what an athlete should look like."

"He's not an athlete, he's a coach," Sloan corrected her, "and a damn good one. Besides, he's not really fat, it's just that incredible stomach of his." He shook his head, wondering why some people's anatomy took such strange turns. "Hard as a medicine ball."

She looked at Sloan incredulously, suddenly recalling talk she had heard about the coach years ago.

"He still encourages students to punch him in the stomach to show how hard it is?" The man had to be close to retirement age himself. Any way you looked at it, he was pushing his luck.

"Encourages?" Sloan laughed again. Hackett had

dared him to do it, but Sloan had refused, saying he'd take the coach's word for it. Others, however, had taken him up on it. "Hell, he urges them. It's a matter of pride. Wants to show all the young up-and-comers that he's still a tough old guy. And he is, too. I wouldn't want to take him on."

Pride, she thought. It always came down to pride. Pride had almost cost her father his life, because he was too proud to go to the doctor and her mother didn't want to rob him of that pride. Pride was a poor substitute for a man's health or his life.

She was being very quiet, Sloan thought. What was she thinking? Had she sensed his feelings? No, he knew Caroline. She would have said something.

He looked at her, grateful that fate had brought her into his life at this time. He'd been feeling restless lately, as if he just didn't belong. Even more so than just after... Sloan silently shrugged away the rest of the thought. All he knew was that he'd been having a difficult time finding a place for himself in his own life—until Caroline arrived.

"Thanks for coming with me tonight, Caroline. I wouldn't have enjoyed myself nearly as much if you hadn't been there."

He meant it, she thought. Meant it just the way it sounded. She had his gratitude, and only that. That should be enough, she reminded herself.

More.

The word moved around her seductively, like a warm current of air.

She tried to shrug it away, and his gratitude with it. "I didn't do anything. Everything at the party would have been the same if I hadn't come with you."

His mouth curved. She still didn't know the difference

she made in people's lives, did she? Not as a doctor, but as a person. Whatever else might have changed in their lives, Caroline was still unassuming.

"Maybe, but it wouldn't have been nearly as cheery and bright." That was it, he thought. Caroline brought laughter and light with her, bathing everything in her path.

She laughed at his choice of words. "So now I'm a detergent?"

The smile on Sloan's face as he spared her a glance before driving on was almost serious. "No, more like sunshine."

Instead of turning left, he turned right at the next light.

Sunshine. He'd called her sunshine. Did he really mean that? She felt her pulse quickening. It took her a moment to realize that he wasn't taking her back to her house.

"Hey, pathfinder," she said playfully, "you're driving toward your house, not mine."

He had taken the turn on purpose. "I know. I thought we'd stop at my place for some coffee." Maybe she was tired, he thought. "Do you mind?"

Caroline leaned against the back of the seat, rotating her shoulders like a cat stretching in the noonday sun. A perfect end to a perfect evening, she thought.

"Mind? Why should I mind? I haven't had my daily Joey and Danny fix yet."

There they ran into a problem. "I'm afraid you're going to have to do without it tonight. They're at my mother's." He saw the quizzical look enter her eyes. "My mother's dog, Beatrix—" he'd always thought that was a strange name for a dog "—had surgery yesterday and my mother didn't want to leave her alone tonight. It's nothing serious, but she babies that animal something awful. The only way I could get her to watch the boys was to bring them to her."

The garage door yawned open as he pulled up the driveway. Sloan drove the car in. He left the door open for a moment as he turned to her.

"They're spending the night there." He was holding his breath, Sloan realized, and he exhaled slowly. His eyes remained on her face.

Anticipation raced over Caroline on tiny little, sneakered feet, but she brushed it aside. She was making something out of nothing again. He was just telling her about baby sitting logistics, nothing more. He wasn't telling her that they were going to be alone. That he had arranged for them to be alone. No planning or arranging had been involved. It had just happened.

Like sunrise every morning. Just something that happened.

She couldn't make the anticipation go away. "Think your mother can handle them?"

He never worried about that. After all, she'd had him and his older brother to practice on. "If I know my mother, she'll let Joey and Danny wear themselves out. All three of them will probably fall asleep in front of the TV, with the dog in the middle. In the morning, when they get up, she'll call it camping out—the civilized way."

There was something endearing about that, Caroline thought. She wondered if they'd be exhausted in the morning. "Good thing tomorrow's Saturday."

"Good thing," he echoed.

Sloan turned on the garage light before pressing the remote to close the door. Taking Caroline's hand, he opened the inner door leading into the family room and walked in.

Caroline looked around the room as Sloan flipped on the lights. "Seems almost eerily quiet," she murmured. She kept expecting the boys to pop out at her at any second.

He took her purse and placed it on the coffee table. She was nervous, he thought. Or was that him? "You feel it, too, eh?"

I feel a lot of things, Sloan. A lot of things I can't tell you about.

She crossed to the kitchen ahead of him. If he wanted coffee, she was going to be the one who made it. Sloan had a tendency to be heavy-handed. His coffee could easily be used as a substitute for asphalt.

"The house is usually full of a joyful noise," she pointed out. The silence made it seem larger somehow, emptier.

She remembered that Sloan had returned here after the funeral. Alone. She'd taken the boys for him, and everyone had gone to his mother's house while he returned here, to roam about by himself.

What was she doing, hoping to find a place in his heart when it was still so full of someone else?

"Sometimes, though," he was saying to her, "it's nice to hear yourself think."

Caroline turned around to face him. There was a strange look in his eyes...one she couldn't quite fathom.

"And what are you thinking?" She wasn't aware that she had whispered the words until she heard herself saying them.

He didn't remember coming to her, didn't remember stopping just an inch shy of where she was standing, but he must have. Because here he was, looking down into her face. "Right now?"

When he looked at her like that, her lips went dry. The words almost stuck to them. "Good place to start."

Was that what this was? he wondered. Was he about to start again? Was he ready to start again?

He didn't know.

He didn't know a great many things lately, except that what he'd said to her in the car was true. She brightened everything she touched. She brightened his life every time she came into it.

She'd asked what he was thinking. He answered honestly. "That I really don't want any coffee."

She had to ask. Knowing she would be disappointed by his answer, she still had to ask. Because she would be disappointed in herself if she didn't. "What is it you do want, Sloan?"

Gently, with just his palms, he skimmed his hands along her bare arms. And felt her shiver. Or was she trembling? There was a world of difference.

"You. I want you, Caroline." And because this *was* Caroline, he could ask, "Am I going crazy?"

If he was, she'd gone there way ahead of him. "Probably," she agreed softly. Her eyes began drifting shut as the sensation of his skin touching hers wound its way through her. She tried to draw it all inside her. To savor. To keep. "But you're not alone," she told him. It was as close as she'd ever come to admitting her secret to him. To admitting that she loved him.

She didn't want this to stop. They were alone, it was probably the only time they would ever be alone, and she didn't want what was happening to stop.

Just this once, she had to take the risk. Whatever the consequences tomorrow, she had to have this one time to call her own.

Opening her eyes, Caroline saw the desire in his. Desire warring with uncertainty. She put her own interpretation on the reasons.

Caroline reached out to tip the scales. "I won't hold you to anything, Sloan. Whatever happens here tonight between us, I won't expect anything in the morning."

She was offering him herself, and asking for nothing in return. He felt humbled. But not enough to draw back. Not on his own. She would have to tell him no for that to happen.

"You never did, did you? No demands, not for your friendship. Not for your loyalty."

He combed his fingers through her hair, framing her face. There was no wild gypsy look there in her eyes, no thin, high cheekbones, no exotic features of any kind to drive a man mad. But there was beauty here, a quiet, classic beauty. Taken separately, each part seemed almost ordinary. Yet somehow, when it all came together, it became extraordinary. The whole was greater than the sum of its parts.

Mrs. Jenkins would have agreed, he thought with a smile.

"What?"

"Nothing. Just an axiom Mrs. Jenkins would have agreed with. Like parallel lines meeting at infinity." Nonsense, he was talking nonsense. To calm the nerves that were beginning to hum again.

"I never will believe that," she murmured as his mouth came down to hers.

"I know."

He wanted her. Heaven help him, he wanted her. Wanted her so badly it almost broke him in two.

He moved his head away. "Caroline, if I hurt you—"

"Shhh," she murmured soothingly. "You won't. No demands, remember? No expectations." She saw the protest forming, born of his guilt. Because of Julie? Because of her? She wouldn't allow either to get in the way. "Makes it easier that way," she whispered. The words feathered along his lips. "No expectations, no disappointments."

She didn't tell him, wouldn't tell him, that there had been disappointments. Such sore disappointments that she'd finally had to leave Bedford to cope with them. To deal with the pain and still remain their friend. Because that friendship was precious to her. So precious that she sacrificed her love for it.

This time it might be the other way around. She might be sacrificing friendship for one night of love.

She couldn't think about it.

He looked into her eyes, beginning to lose himself by inches. "You really are amazing."

"Show me." The entreaty caressed him like the hand of a lover, urging him on. "Just this once, show me how amazing you think I am." Her eyes danced with just a little humor, hypnotizing him. "Put your money where your mouth is."

He drew her closer, so close he could feel her heart beat against his. "I'll do better than that,"

She could feel herself sinking into him, becoming lost. "Oh?"

He didn't answer. Instead, he sealed his mouth to hers and sent every nerve impulse within her racing.

Running for cover. Running toward him, and the ecstasy she had always known would be there.

The rest seemed to happen in a haze. A haze of heat, of desire. A haze composed of a feeling so strong, he was surrounded by it. A feeling of homecoming.

Caroline's acceptance of this turn in their relationship, her willingness to give herself, completely stripped him of the uncertainty that had kept him shackled. There was no turning back.

He ran to meet his destiny.

It was as if he'd opened a door, entering only to find that the door led to an abyss, not a room. A bottomless abyss. He tumbled down, with no floor to break his fall, with nothing to stop it.

He fell. And gloried in the rush, the exhilaration that coursed through his veins as he tumbled head over heels.

At first, he only kissed her, kissed her over and over again, feasting on her rich mouth, each kiss deeper than the one that had come before. Building. Building his excitement, his anticipation. Building, too, the incredible feeling of contentment that went hand in hand with this insane desire that had seized hold of him.

They tumbled onto the sofa, too caught up in each other to even care whether it was the sofa, or the floor, that ultimately cradled them.

It was happening. It was really happening. He wasn't just kissing her, he was going to make love with her. The wish she'd first made so many years ago was finally being granted.

Talk about a delay factor.

The whimsical thought nudged its way forward, making her smile.

He felt her mouth curving beneath his, and raised his head, confused. But she wasn't laughing at him, or even at them. He knew that smile. Even though she'd changed in a hundred different ways, he knew that smile. It was delight.

He tucked a hair behind her ear, finding an odd sort of comfort in doing something so mundanely familiar in the midst of lovemaking. "What is it? Why are you smiling like that? Like a cat savoring a canary."

Oh, no, he wasn't going to drag this out of her. Not until she was ready to tell him. "It's a secret. Someday, I'll let you in on it."

Maybe.

"Friends don't have secrets from each other." Sloan shifted his weight, afraid he was pressing her into the sofa.

"Yeah, they do."

Then, before he could press her any further, Caroline did the only thing she could. She twined her arms around his neck and pulled his mouth to hers.

This had to take place before she woke up and discovered it was only just another dream.

There was no more time for talk. Not when he couldn't readily form any coherent words. If there were words, they would be those of an apology, for in his heart he knew he was taking advantage. Of the moment, of her. But he couldn't help himself. And he didn't want to apologize. He wanted her.

Over and over again, his mouth worshiped hers, feeding on the sweetness he found there. And all the while, his senses swirled around him, taking things in with the wonder of a cloistered child let out into the sun for the first time.

Their bodies were sealed so close, transcending the barriers of clothes, time and space, there wasn't even room for a breath.

She could feel the heat as it penetrated, radiating from him to her. Feel the length of his body in every place where it touched hers.

Arching, she wanted more, wanted him to take her wantonly, completely and forever. Sloan would be her first, and no matter what came afterward, he would be her last. She would be his forever.

She already was in her heart.

It had been so long since he felt like this, like an awkward teenager with his first girl. This was a hell of a time to travel down that nostalgic road. He cursed himself inwardly as he fumbled with the zipper at the back of her dress. Any second, it was going to catch the fabric and get stuck. Or, worse, nip her flesh.

He was having trouble. Why did that strike her as being so hopelessly sweet? Arching for him, her eyes on his, Caroline reached behind her and sent the zipper sliding down to its base.

She wasn't wearing a bra.

Caroline settled back, her smile deceptively calm, her heart hammering something that sounded vaguely like the "Anvil Chorus." The dress lay over her body, a soft covering he had only to blow away. Beneath it, she had only a scrap of nylon clinging to her hips.

Like a man in a dream, he took her into his arms again and kissed her lips. First slowly, then ardently and with a passion that threatened to explode, shelling them both.

The fabric slipped down. Away. Gathering along her waist, trapped between them. He urged it away, and with it, the last barrier that hid her from him. It was all he could do not to snatch the flimsy bit of nylon away, but to ease it down, gently.

And then his breath caught in his throat, Sloan looked down at her nude body. At the small, firm breasts that begged for his touch. The taut, flat belly that quivered ever so slightly. His heart slammed against his chest. She was beautiful.

He filled his hands with her, trailing his fingers along skin that felt as smooth, as silken, as the first pristine snow of the season.

She needed to feel him, to touch him the way he was

touching her. To burn her palms across his flesh the way he was doing across hers. Anxious, with movements far more self-assured than she was, Caroline tugged at his jacket, pulling it from his shoulders.

He raised his head, an inkling of a smile playing along his lips. "I guess I am a little overdressed."

Sloan shrugged the jacket from his arms, then unbuttoned his shirt, pulling it from his waistband. His eyes never left her, drinking in the sight of her lying there, so perfect it made him ache just to look at her. The shirt was discarded on the floor.

She could feel her loins tightening, longing.

When he got to the notch holding his belt in place, Sloan took her hands in his and drew them to the buckle. Gently, with just the press of his fingers, he urged her to complete the job.

Excitement roared through her like a runaway train. She'd gone through all the appropriate classes in medical school and her residency, and there was no part of the human anatomy that remained a mystery to her. It didn't matter. The anticipation of his body broke new ground, whispered of promises unspoken.

What she had seen in medical school belonged to the professional Caroline. It had never touched the private woman she was.

Her hands shook as she undressed him.

Eager, he thought, she was eager for this union. Watching her fueled his own excitement, until he was lost in its folds. It was all he could do not to take over and peel his trousers off himself.

It felt better when she did it.

Clothing discarded, they explored each other's bodies with the wonder of two who had never been at this junction before. Textures were tested, tastes cataloged and absorbed. The gathering of sensations proceeded at increasingly higher temperatures.

Until, with the cushions of the sofa bearing silent witness, the whirlwind spiraled to its peak.

He kept his eyes on her face, anticipating a sign that, at the last minute, she wanted to back away from this madness that had seized them both; his hands joined with hers. Sloan slowly began to sheathe himself in her.

And abruptly stopped, his eyes widening, as a shaft of reality was fired through the haze of the powerful dream that kept him prisoner.

"Caroline—?"

Too late. It was too late for him to stop. Too late to call an end to this. She couldn't bear it if he stopped now.

She reached for him, guiding him where he wouldn't have forced his way, even now. If there was pain, she was prepared for it. And it was a small price to pay in exchange for what she received.

He was lost, unable to do the right thing, unable to brace himself and withdraw, the way decency demanded that he should.

Not when she was like this.

Her hips were moving urgently against his, calling for a response, in a rhythm that was already drumming through his body.

Lips finding hers once again, Sloan let the rhythm take him away.

Joined, they finished the journey together. Just the way she'd always dreamed of.

Chapter 12

The warmth of the afterglow broke apart as guilt slith-
ered in on its belly, taking its place. Encircling him.
Squeezing him like an anaconda. Sloan silently shifted
his weight away from Caroline. But the damage had already been done.

Damn it, he hadn't known, would have never
guessed...

Sloan dragged air slowly back into his lungs, trying
to find a way to approach the subject. To tell her he was
sorry.

There was no way.

She wasn't saying anything, and it cut through him
like the edge of a well-honed knife. He didn't want to
lose her. Caroline's friendship meant everything to him.
Sloan closed his eyes. Well, he had just sacrificed everything for an hour's pleasure.

Oh no, he wasn't saying anything. He wasn't even

looking at her. Was he angry with her? Disappointed? Sorry he had ever started any of this?

The questions burned their way into every corner of her mind.

Trying desperately for composure, Caroline pulled her discarded dress to her. It took every scrap of courage she had to force herself to look at him.

He could feel her eyes. Sloan opened his own and looked at her. Was that an accusation he saw there? No, that wasn't Caroline. She didn't accuse, even when she had the right to. But there was hurt in her eyes. He'd hurt her. Not knowing was no excuse.

"Why didn't you tell me?"

Self-consciousness yanked away the last threads of contentment that had, only seconds ago, been wrapped around her.

Defiant, she lifted her chin. "What?"

What? How could she pretend she didn't know what he was talking about?

"That you've never…that you're…" Stymied, Sloan fumbled over his own tongue, cursing himself inwardly.

So that was what this was about. He *was* disappointed because she wasn't experienced enough for him. Caroline felt as if someone had dropped a bucket of ice water on her.

"What? That I've never skied? That I'm type AB positive?" She could see confusion mingled with the anger in his face. "See, you don't know that about me, either. Those are just some of the things I've never told you because they never came up, never had a place in any of our conversations."

"It's not the same thing." Angry with himself, he bit the words off.

"No? All right, just where was I supposed to stick

that little tidbit in? 'Hi, Sloan, by the way, did I tell you I'm still a virgin?'" Had she really misjudged him that much all these years? She'd just given him her heart, as well as her body, and he was upset because he'd had no advance warning that the woman he was about to make love with was a novice. "There *was* no opening for that piece of information anywhere. And it's not exactly something I wanted to plaster all over a billboard."

Caroline rose, backing up as she gathered her things to her. All she wanted to do was get dressed and leave. She could walk home from here.

Her denial didn't change anything, didn't negate the guilt he felt over stealing something precious away from her. "There *was* every opening. You could have told me before anything happened."

She turned and glared at him. "I didn't know anything *was* going to happen."

I hoped, but I didn't know. She bit back the hurt. She didn't want it to end on this note. It couldn't, not if they were to ever look at each other again. Her voice softened.

"And I don't think you did, either." She looked at him and knew she was right. "So what happens now? Do you penalize me twelve points? Does that make me a minus three?" She shifted the bundle in her arms to keep her shoes from falling on the floor.

Her question caught him so totally off guard, Sloan could only stare at her, feeling like a dim-witted idiot. "What are you talking about?"

Everything was getting so muddled. And it should have been so wonderful. Sloan had made love with her. After all these years, he'd made love with her.

"I don't know." She lifted her shoulders and let them drop helplessly. "I'm assuming that you're upset about my 'untried state' because the first time you make love with someone in over a year, you wind up being disappointed." She swallowed. "Because I have no technique."

Was that what she thought? Didn't she know him better than that? "You're way off base. I'm not looking for technique. I—" He stopped abruptly as something else she'd said played itself back to him. "How do you know it's the first time?"

His question made her smile. There was absolutely no doubt in her mind that Sloan had remained true to Julie's memory.

"Because it's you. Because you never slept around. It wasn't in your nature." Her eyes softened as some of her hurt siphoned off, and with it, her defensive anger. She loved him, she thought. No matter how he felt about her, she loved him. That would always be true. "Because your heart is pure, Galahad, and you have the strength of ten."

Was she quoting a line from an old text? His professional pride got the better of him. "I don't recognize that. What's it from?"

She covered her heart with her hand. "Here, Sloan. It's from right here."

Her answer humbled him. Sloan reached for her hand, bringing it to his lips. He pressed a kiss to her knuckles. She deserved so much more than he had just given her.

"Caroline, I'm sorry. I'm not upset because you're a virgin. That's absurd." How could she think that little of him? Or was it nerves that made her believe that he could be so insensitive? Maybe there was still more of the old Caroline left in there than appearances would lead him to believe. "I'm upset because you didn't tell me. Because I didn't know when I took you." His eyes touched her face, caressing it. "Because your first time is supposed to be special."

The man was even denser than she'd thought. And sweeter. "What makes you think it wasn't?"

Her heart was in her eyes.

He couldn't resist. Had he been made out of stone, Sloan couldn't have resisted her, couldn't have resisted the look that bid him come to her.

He couldn't resist, but he could offer her an escape route. "Caroline..."

She didn't want to hear it. Not any more apologies, not any more words. She just wanted to taste his mouth again, to satisfy, oh-so-temporarily, the craving that she knew would never be fully satisfied.

Caroline let her clothes slip from her hands. They rained down in a heap at her feet as she placed her fingertips to his lips.

"You do talk too much, Professor, you know that?" Tilting her head back, she brought her mouth up to his. He met her halfway.

There was nothing left to talk about.

Only to feel.

Caroline stayed the night. A night she knew would remain with her for the rest of her life. Not because they'd made love through half of it, although that part had been exquisitely perfect. No, it was what happened afterward, in the wee hours of the night, a time when the darkest fears rose up to haunt a person.

There was no fear. There was only him. She lay there in Sloan's arms, silently listening to him breathe evenly as he slept. It was the sound of music to her.

For just that tiny island of time, she could pretend that the past seventeen years had been hers, that they hadn't belonged to a friend she loved better than a sister. She could pretend that the heart of the man sleeping beside her belonged to her, as did his children.

Just for tonight.

Warmed by his steady breath, cocooned within her fantasy, Caroline curled her body into his and watched the shadows chase each other on the ceiling for a very long time before her eyes finally began to close. Her last thought was that, with luck, morning would take an abnormally long time to arrive.

She had meant to be gone by first light, she really had. Because she was desperately afraid of seeing even the slightest sign of regret in his eyes. She wanted nothing to mar the memory of the night they'd had together.

Morning might have always been her favorite time of day, but not today. Daylight had a way of harshly exposing some things that could exist only in the shadow of night. She didn't want what had happened last night to fade away when exposed to the dawn. Not yet. She knew it would happen soon enough.

But because she'd lain awake half the night, Caroline slept through the first rays of dawn creeping into the room. Slept through the almost martial-arts, certainly noisy, fight engaged in by two scrub jays somewhere out on Sloan's lawn.

It wasn't until she felt him rise from the bed that she woke up.

Though she was dead to the world at large, it was as if every fiber of her body were attuned to him. Set to go off when he moved.

Instantly awake, she debated feigning sleep, just to hang on to her fantasy a little longer. If he thought she was asleep, he couldn't tell her that he had regrets about his behavior after all.

But that was the cowardly way. The old way, belonging to the old Caroline. And for Caroline, there was no turning back.

Stretching, she allowed herself one last comfortable moment in bed before she got up. One last moment in his bed as his lover. He'd brought her up here after they all but wore out the sofa, saying she deserved at least a little comfort.

She didn't care about comfort. All she cared about was making love with him. But she couldn't say that, couldn't weigh him down with the burden of her love, so she had come to his bedroom and made love in his bed. And lost her heart all over again. There wasn't even a tiny piece left for her to salvage.

Sloan turned when he heard her moving. He'd been trying to be quiet. She looked so peaceful, he didn't want to disturb her.

Sunlight from the open window bathed her in golden hues. He felt his gut tightening all over again. When had he become so damn insatiable? "Good morning."

She tried to study his face, but he was standing by the bureau, in the shadows. She felt like a tightrope walker working without a net.

"Is it?"

Somewhere, whoever had written the code book of behavior for the woman of the nineties was clutching her stomach at the unabashed hope that was seeking a toehold within her. In her defense, Caroline had never learned the rules of the game. There had never been a reason. She'd never been a player before.

There shouldn't be this awkward feeling, he thought,

not with Caroline. He banished it as he pulled on an old pair of jeans.

"Well, the sun is shining outside." He crossed the room and sat down at the edge of the bed, on her side. Sloan looked down at her face. "How's it doing inside?"

"I think it's shining on this side." Feeling as if she were on tenterhooks, Caroline sat up against the headboard, pulling the sheet up and tucking it around her breasts.

She thought. She didn't know. Sloan reached for her hand, wrapping his fingers around it. "About last night—" he began hesitantly.

"Nothing's changed," Caroline said quickly, so afraid that it had. For the worse. Her fears of losing his friendship returned, in overwhelming proportions.

His eyebrows drew together in an expression of mild bewilderment. She was too intelligent to believe that. "A whole hell of a lot has changed, Caroline. I know for a fact now that you don't do this with all your friends."

She looked down at their joined hands, trying to quell the nervousness in the pit of her stomach. "We can pretend it never happened."

He didn't understand. Was she having regrets after all? "Why would we want to do that?"

She shrugged, almost losing the sheet. She clutched at it. "If it makes you uncomfortable with me—" She began again. "If it means losing a friend—"

He moved closer, drawn by her vulnerability. He was attracted to her strength, but it was her vulnerability that held him, touched him. He hadn't meant for any of this to happen. But now that it had, he was glad that it had. Glad he had shared the moment with Caroline.

Sloan feathered his fingers through her hair. "You

didn't lose a friend, Caroline. But I'm not sure if you gained anything." He honestly had no idea where any of this was going, or even whether it was going anywhere at all. "I'm—"

"Going to be late picking up the boys." It was too soon to talk about this. It was too new, too fresh.

For now, it was enough that she hadn't lost his friendship. If there was anything to be built, they could build from there.

Avoiding his eyes, she scooted over to the opposite side of the bed and got out, the sheet wrapped around her. She felt like an encumbered snail. "I had planned on being gone before you woke up, anyway."

He watched her as she moved, cocooned in a plaid sheet. He'd slept beneath that sheet countless times. It had never seemed sexy to him before. "Like a dream?"

Something in his voice made her turn around. "A dream? Is that what last night was?" Did that mean it was over, the way dreams were in the light of the morning sun?

He nodded. "In a way. A beautiful, forbidden dream." Rising, he crossed to her and took her hand again. Who was this person before him, this person who set the blood in his veins on fire? He wasn't sure.

"I've known you most of my life, Caroline, and it occurs to me that I really don't know you at all. At least, not the way I thought I did."

And that was a good thing, she thought, reading the look in his eyes. "It's those hidden gifts I told you about."

He took her into his arms, pressing a kiss to her temple. It felt so right, holding her like this. "Anything else I should know about?"

Caroline felt herself heating already. "I'll let you know if I think of anything."

"You know," he said, pressing a kiss to her other temple, "my mother likes to sleep in on Saturdays."

Her head dropped back as his mouth skimmed the hollow of her throat. It was getting difficult to breathe. Difficult to think again. She reveled in the sensation. Thinking was highly overrated, anyway. "Think the boys'll let her?"

He slipped his hands in beneath the sheet, cupped her bottom and held her to him. Her little moan of pleasure went right through him.

"I figure that's her problem. Me, I've got my hands full."

She touched her tongue to her lips. Desire was searing through her. "I noticed."

Still holding her to him, he resisted the urge to tear the sheet away. It was more tantalizing to go slow. "What about you?"

Her head was spinning. She spread her palms over his chest and moved them along his skin slowly. Hard muscle tantalized her skin. "I could have my hands full, all right."

He grinned. She'd misunderstood. "I mean, do you have to be anywhere?"

Slowly, she moved her head from side to side. "Nowhere but where I am." It was too early for responsibility, too early to do for anyone but herself. This hour of the morning belonged to her alone. And she meant to make the most of it.

"Good enough."

Sloan covered her mouth with his, excitement drenching him. Just talking to her, knowing she had on nothing but her perfume beneath the sheet, aroused him.

He would have thought that arousal wasn't possible anymore, not after the night they'd had. He had considered himself all but spent by the time he drifted off to sleep, holding her in his arms. He'd obviously miscalculated.

It was equally apparent that his long months of complete celibacy hadn't erased all traces of desire; they had only allowed it to sit in a dark, lonely place and grow to extreme proportions.

Or maybe it was just this woman who brought all this out in him.

He hadn't a clue.

Her face framed in his hands, Sloan kissed her mouth over and over again, making himself crazy. Where was this going? he asked himself again. It was happening so fast. So fast, after so many years.

"Caroline," he whispered honestly. "I don't know what to make of this—"

Why did he have to try so hard to analyze it? Very few things could stand analysis. Why couldn't he just let it be?

Her arms around his neck, she brought his head down to hers.

"Then don't try to make anything of it. Mrs. Jenkins told us to enjoy what life gives us." A mischievous, seductive smile curved her mouth. "I make it a point never to question anything a teacher tells me."

He laughed, softly nipping her lower lip between his teeth before outlining her lips with his tongue. "I could use a dozen students like you in class."

Her eyes hazed by desire, she moved her body urgently against Sloan's. "I think maybe one might be enough for you."

As long as that one was her. Desire took another bite out of him. "I think you're right."

The sheet slid down to the floor, pooling over their bare feet. She lowered her gaze, taking it in. Taking in the fact that he was still wearing his jeans. "I think you're overdressed again."

He wanted her to undress him. To feel her fingers flutter lightly along his skin. To feel her lips against it, quenching the fire.

The very thought made his body tighten. Harden. "Then why don't you do something about it?"

Anticipation, alive and well and even greater than it had been yesterday, leaped through her. "Like I said, I make it a point never to question anything a teacher tells me."

Careful to keep her hands steady, she slid the metal button from its hole. She didn't want anything to label her a novice in his eyes again.

The jeans continued to cling to his hips.

The way she wanted to.

His eyes urged her on. "Never knew you not to finish something you started."

Once, Caroline thought. *Just once. I fell in love with you and didn't see it through to the end.*

"I wouldn't want to develop any bad habits this late in my life." Her hands on either side of his hips, she slowly coaxed his jeans down his hips.

Her head fell back as Sloan pressed his lips to her throat.

It was hard keeping her mind on what she was doing when thoughts were winking in and out of her head like a firefly searching for somewhere to alight.

Her hands felt cool against his flesh. His breath caught

in his throat, even as he kissed her. She was making him crazy.

It was even better this time.

There were no awkward doubts humming in the back of his mind, making him afraid that at the last moment he'd made a mistake. Or that she would withdraw, saying that the mistake was hers. This time, he was sure. Sure that they both knew what they wanted.

And what they wanted was this moment, served hot, savored slowly.

And he did. He savored her. Savored every delicious nuance, every fragrance, every flavor. Over and over again, until it was indelibly imprinted on his mind. On his soul.

And still he wanted more.

More of her, more of this insane rush that possessed him each time he took her.

More.

Sloan pushed her back against the bed. She stretched, like a cat, urging him to join her. He didn't wait for a second invitation.

As sunlight caressed her body, urging him to do the same, Sloan brought her to him. Their limbs tangled in a primitive dance, he lost himself in the power of the sensations that swept over him.

He wanted to go slow. Began with the intent of going slow, of sampling and feasting on something that was now familiar. But he was mistaken. It wasn't familiar. Daylight had made it different. Special. Incredibly enticing.

He couldn't go slow, couldn't hold back.

Unable to help himself, trapped in a rhythm he felt rather than heard, he began to move more quickly, to race to a hidden finish line.

He was lost all over again, imprisoned by his desires. Imprisoned by her.

She was right; morning really was the best time. Instead of exposing, daylight highlighted, warmed, caressed with a gentle and loving hand.

As gentle as the hand that had caressed her through the night of lovemaking.

From every conceivable place within her, feelings rose to swirl around Caroline, setting off tiny depth charges. She wanted him to feel like this. As if loving her could empower him. She wanted to give, not just receive. And to make him feel as insanely happy as he made her.

She felt exhilarated. Excited. Both master and slave of the very same feelings. That was what she wanted for him. To feel that. To feel as if he could touch the sky.

Most of all, she wanted him to love her.

"Never satisfied," a small voice whispered along the perimeter of her mind, so clearly that she could have sworn she'd heard it.

"What?" Blinking, Caroline looked at Sloan. "Did you say something?"

He shook his head, a smile spreading his generous mouth. "Not me. It's hard to talk when you're swallowing your tongue."

"Are you? Do I make you do that, Sloan? Make you swallow your own tongue?"

"Yes." His hands swept hypnotically over the length of her body. "There's no other explanation why I can't find it." He rolled her onto her back. "Why I can't even summon a coherent thought that doesn't begin and end with you."

She embraced his words, wanting to believe them with her whole heart and soul. "Nothing wrong with that."

He marveled as he watched her curve into the sensation his hand created within her. Watched her curve into him. He meant to tantalize her, but he succeeded in undoing himself, as well.

Her eyes grew smoky with desire, her pupils large enough for him to lose himself in.

Exciting her excited him.

So this was what they meant by a win-win situation, Sloan thought. That was what he had here.

For now.

But now, he thought as he brought her to him, was all that counted. All they had. All they ever could hope to ask for.

Wanting to drive himself into Caroline, holding back so that he wouldn't hurt her, Sloan took her again. And, in taking, lost himself.

Willingly.

Chapter 13

The temptation to remain in bed with Caroline, her body warm against his, was overwhelming. But he had a life waiting for him beyond the boundaries of sheets that had gotten so tangled. So did she. Sloan had to get moving, if he was to have any hopes of not falling behind schedule.

He allowed himself one quick, fleeting kiss and then forced himself out of bed. "I've got another rehearsal scheduled this morning."

Her eyes half-closed, Caroline ran the tip of her tongue along her lips. She could taste him, she thought, the flavor wafting through her. How long would it last? She knew the answer to that. Not nearly long enough.

"I want to stop by the hospital to see how my dad's doing." So far, the prognosis was optimistic. "Dr. Shaffer thinks he might be able to come home as early as Monday." There was a lot to do before Monday. Visiting nurses to schedule, therapists to interview.

And all she wanted to do was stay here, warm and safe within Sloan's arms.

She was becoming positively decadent, Caroline thought, a wanton smile curving her mouth as her eyes drifted shut again.

"That's great." Sloan paused for a second, watching the smile trace her lips. There was that tug, he thought, deep within his gut again. The last time he'd felt something like that...

"Caroline?"

Something in his voice roused her. She opened her eyes and looked at him. "Hmm?"

Sloan bit the words back. Once they were out, he couldn't take them back. Couldn't erase them. What he thought he was feeling was probably just residue from the night before, nothing more. No reason to give any more weight to it.

"Nothing," he murmured, turning toward the bathroom. "I'm going to take a quick shower before I pick up Joey and Danny. It promises to be a very long day." The telephone rang just as he was about to close the door. "Get that for me, will you?"

"What if it's your mother?" She figured it was a reasonable question. Would he want his mother knowing she'd spent the night?

He grinned. His mother would probably do handsprings if she knew he'd ventured out into the social world again. She'd started in on him about that nearly six months ago. "Tell her you're the Avon lady, showing me a new line of products."

"That should go over well," Caroline murmured to herself. The sound of his laughter as he closed the door warmed her. She loved hearing him laugh. It was a deep, rich sound that was supremely comforting, like a warm coat on a freezing winter day.

The phone rang again, demanding attention. Stretching, Caroline reached across the bed and picked up the receiver. She held it to her ear as she sat up, bringing her knees to her.

There was probably a law against feeling this good, she thought with a silly grin.

"Hello, Walters residence." She heard a sharp intake of breath, but nothing else followed in its wake. Listening, Caroline thought she detected soft music in the background, but she wasn't sure. "Hello? Is someone there?"

The sound of a receiver being slammed into its cradle was her only reply. Shrugging, Caroline replaced the telephone.

With a languid sigh, she swung her legs out and got up. Time wasn't going to stop for her, no matter how much she wanted it to. Forcing herself to move quickly, she gathered her clothes together and got dressed.

She'd just zipped up her dress when the door to the bathroom opened. A wall of wispy steam followed as Sloan walked out. His hair was damp, curling along his neck, and there were a few stray drops still clinging to his chest. *Lucky drops,* she thought. A bath towel hung precariously knotted at his waist as he absently ran his hand over the day old stubble on his chin.

The man was a moving portrait of raw sex.

All her life, Caroline had held herself in check. But it was like the little boy taking his finger out of the hole in the dam. Once that happened, there was no holding back the water that came rushing out. She felt insatiable, wanting him again.

"Who was on the phone?" he asked. A deliciously

mischievous smile lifted the corners of his mouth. "Was it my mother?"

He didn't mind, she thought. Didn't mind if his mother knew. The realization warmed her.

She shook her head. "Whoever it was hung up. Must've been a wrong number, although they didn't ask for anyone." That was a little strange, she thought. Most people asked for someone before they realized they had the wrong number.

Another wrong number. This was getting to be an annoying habit. Sloan moved back into the bathroom and reached for his comb. "They never do."

Knowing she should be elsewhere—at the very least in the kitchen getting breakfast—Caroline followed him into the bathroom, curiosity urging her on.

He smelled of water and soap, some manly, woodsy fragrance. It took effort to keep her mind on her question. "What do you mean by that? Have you gotten these calls before?"

He combed the hair out of his eyes, then took out his razor and shaving cream. He hated shaving, but the alternative wasn't very appealing to him, either.

Sloan nodded in reply to her question. "For the last week or so." The calls came at all hours, always the same. Someone would call, then listen to him say hello several times before hanging up. "They're getting annoying, really."

Caroline frowned, leaning against the doorjamb. "How many calls?"

Sloan spread shaving cream along one cheekbone. "A handful." He paused to think. "Maybe fifteen or so." The razor sliced through the foam. "I figure it's either some idiot who can't figure out he's got the wrong number, or an obscene caller in training, in which case they've really got the wrong number."

He thought it was funny, but she didn't. Fifteen phone calls were not an accident. Someone was obviously doing this on purpose. "Why?"

"Well, men don't get obscene phone calls. Only women do. I can't see a woman doing that sort of thing to a man. It doesn't make any sense."

She wanted to know more about this anonymous caller. Did Sloan have something to really be concerned about? "What did you mean by obscene caller in training?"

"Because nothing's ever said. Someone just listens to me say hello a couple of times and then hangs up. No husky-voiced scenario, not even any heavy breathing. Maybe it's some guy, hoping to luck out and have a woman pick up."

She didn't think it was that simple. "If that were the case, whoever it was would have gone to town when I answered. Instead, they slammed down the phone."

That struck a familiar chord. "The only time that happened to me was when I thought it was you calling."

She looked at him quizzically.

"I said, 'Caroline, is that you?' and then, bam, the receiver was pitched into the cradle. My ear was ringing for ten minutes."

It had to be a woman. A woman who was upset at hearing Sloan mistake her for someone else. A woman who became angry when she heard another woman on the line.

Bits and pieces began to dovetail in Caroline's mind. "Do you think it might be Allison?"

Finished, he rinsed out his razor, then shook it off.

The possibility that it might be someone he knew had never occurred to him.

"I doubt it." Sloan reached for the towel on the rack and wiped his face. "Besides," he added as he slung the towel over the side of the shower stall, "how would she get my number? I'm unlisted."

Caroline took down the towel mechanically and folded it neatly, then placed it back on the rack. "Never underestimate the power of a woman in love."

He grinned to himself. She wasn't even conscious of what she was doing, he thought. Caroline was behaving like a wife. He'd missed that sort of thing, those tiny touches that made a house a home.

He'd had a wife, Sloan reminded himself sternly. That part of his life was over. He forced his mind back on the topic. It obviously worried Caroline, but as far as he was concerned, it was all harmless.

"She's not a woman," he insisted, "and we agreed that Allison had a crush on me, nothing more."

He didn't remember what it was like, did he? To be that age and love someone so much that it ached? "We see it as a crush. She sees it as undying love."

The description made him intensely uncomfortable. He wasn't ready to concede. "Okay, how would she get my number?"

That seemed easy enough to her. "Does she volunteer to work in the admissions office?"

"As a matter of fact, no. Allison told me when she tried out for the play that she usually liked hanging around the school as little as possible, but that I made things so much fun, she was making an exception." But even as he said it, he realized just how dense he had been. The signs had been there for him all along.

What other signs had he been oblivious to? he wondered.

Caroline gave it some more thought. "Okay, no volunteering. Still that doesn't mean that she doesn't know someone who does volunteer there. They could snoop around—or..." She looked up sharply. It was so simple, she might have missed it entirely. "You said the students took turns looking out for Danny and Joey when you brought them to rehearsal."

"Right." What was she getting at? "So?"

"So?" Before his eyes, Caroline was transformed into a dewy-eyed innocent. Sporting a bright, guileless smile, she bent down, pretending to address a child in a terminally sugary voice. "Gee, you're a bright boy, Joey. I bet you even know your address and phone number." Caroline straightened, giving Sloan a triumphant look. "And Joey, to prove that she's right about his brain capacity, recites it for her. Allison commits it to memory." Caroline spread her hands. "End of mystery."

Sloan turned the explanation over in his mind. She had a point. He would have never thought of that. "Are all women that devious?"

She hooked her fingers playfully on the towel around his middle. The feel of his taut skin sent shivers running through her. With just the slightest of movements, the towel could be on its way to communing with the tile. It took willpower for her to remind herself that they were just having a conversation and that they both had to be somewhere else soon.

"To a lesser or greater degree, yes." With superhuman effort, she withdrew her hand and stepped back, giving him clear access to his closet. "It's part of our initiation into the sisterhood. We have to be more devious, to make up for the fact that we're the 'weaker' sex.''

He pulled out a pair of comfortable jeans, tossing them on the bed. A pale gray pullover shirt and underwear followed. ''Weaker, my butt.''

She couldn't help the laugh that rose in her throat. ''I didn't notice that it was particularly weak. You've got a very cute butt.''

He looked at her in surprise. Caroline continued to be a revelation. ''I didn't think you'd pay attention to something like that.''

He really was an innocent, wasn't he? ''All women pay attention to butts, Sloan. Some of us just don't admit it, that's all.''

Without the slightest bit of embarrassment, he let the towel drop and pulled on his briefs, then his jeans. It amused him that this woman who had turned into a firebrand in his arms last night now discreetly looked away. Or pretended to. She was an enigma, all right.

''I guess there's a lot about you I didn't know.''

She looked over her shoulder at him, the very picture of what he would have labeled a temptress if he was researching a piece of eighteenth-century literature. ''Just enough to make me interesting.''

He was torn. Torn between taking her in his arms again and doing what was expected of him: picking up his sons and heading to rehearsal. It was a tough call. Though it was completely out of character for him, he began to weaken.

Caroline could see what he was thinking. Could see it, and hugged it to her like a secret love letter. As he reached for her, she made the decision for him, though it wasn't any easier for her than it was for him.

She placed her hand on his chest. ''Your mother might

get antsy and bring Joey and Danny here instead of waiting for you to come by. I don't think you want her walking in on us."

It was one thing for his mother to find out that his libido had been resurrected; it was another to see it in action. "One thing I know for sure—I can rely on your clear thinking. Come out in the kitchen, I'll make you breakfast."

"Oh, no, you don't." She hurried after him. "*I'll* make breakfast."

He laughed, slipping his arm around her shoulders. "I was hoping you'd say that."

Her father's hospital room was a far cheerier place when she walked into it than it had been a week ago. The transformation had little to do with the myriad of flower arrangements that were strategically scattered throughout the room, perching on any available flat surface. The change had come about because the feeling of fear had left. That, and her father had some of his old zest for life back. Even the heavy bandages around his head didn't detract from that.

It was good to see him like this, Caroline thought. She glanced at her mother, sitting at his bedside. Good to see *both* of them like this. They were holding hands like newlyweds.

"I can leave and give you two some privacy," Caroline offered, pivoting on her heel and eyeing the door.

"Not a bad idea." Joshua laughed. He looked at his daughter. He knew he owed his life to her, as much as to the surgeon who had performed the operation. His eyes narrowed as he scrutinized her face. "You look like the cat that ate the canary."

Because Sloan was on her mind, she flushed, knowing

it only made things worse. "I don't know what you're talking about." Did it show that much?

Joshua exchanged glances with his wife. He grinned. "Not only ate it, but came back for seconds."

She didn't think this was the right time to tell them about Sloan. Or whether there was even something to tell. There was still so much unsaid, so much unsettled. She was afraid it would all disappear if she so much as mentioned it to someone else.

She smoothed out the edge of her father's white blanket. "I'm just happy that you're well, that's all."

Joshua snorted. "Don't try to snow your old man, honey. I've done enough of that myself to know when someone is standing over me with a snow shovel." Because he loved her, he was prepared to welcome whoever made his daughter happy with open arms. He'd been waiting for that to happen for a long time. "Who's responsible for that look on your face?"

Though caught up in the grip of despair, Wanda hadn't been completely oblivious to what was going on around her. "She's been seeing a lot of Sloan Walters."

Joshua's smile widened. This was better than he'd hoped. He actually liked Sloan Walters. "Sloan, eh?"

She really didn't want this getting out. Her parents had a network of friends who could spread a story faster than any news service.

"We're friends, Dad," she said firmly. "It's only natural to spend some time with him, catching up on old times."

She might be trying to fool herself, but she wasn't fooling him. "Are you laying groundwork for any new times?"

Caroline sighed. When her father got an idea in his head, it was stuck there as if it were cemented down.

Afraid he'd see something in her eyes, she turned away. "It's not like that."

"Isn't it?" He caught her hand and forced her to look at him. "Uh-huh."

For a man one week out of surgery, he had a powerful grip. The thought gladdened her, even as she asked defensively, "What 'uh-huh'?"

He saw all he needed to. He always could read her like a book. "Make sure he's good to you, Carrie. You deserve the best."

"Dad, there's nothing going on between Sloan and me." She saw that the protest fell on deaf ears. There was no lying to him. "Or, if it is, it's nothing permanent. Sloan's still in love with Julie." And when push came to shove, she couldn't compete with a memory. It was too difficult.

Wanda gently touched her arm. "Did he tell you that?"

Caroline shrugged helplessly. "Not in so many words." He never let the conversation go there, steering it away from any mention of Julie. But she knew him; she could read between the lines.

Still tethered to one remaining intravenous bottle, Joshua sat up. "Then don't put any in his mouth, Carrie. Besides, a man can't live in the past, especially if he has kids to look out for." His money was on Caroline. His daughter had turned into an independent, strong, beautiful young woman. A man would have to be blind to walk away from her. "Sloan Walters never struck me as a recluse. And if he's buried himself a little in the past, help him dig himself out. You'll be doing him a favor. And me."

Caroline didn't quite follow the logic. "You? Why you?"

Her mother supplied the answer. "Your dad always wanted grandchildren to spoil."

"Oh, like she didn't want any," Joshua said teasingly, taking his wife's hand again.

Wanda placed her other hand over his, stroking it lovingly. "Right now, I can't wait until you come home, so I can spoil you."

Feeling like a young buck again, Joshua inclined his head toward his wife, comically raising and lowering his graying brows. "I'll hold you to that."

This was what she wanted, Caroline thought. The kind of love that was at the heart of her parents' marriage. Sure, there were things wrong, things that weren't perfect in their marriage and needed fixing. But all that could be dealt with, because there was love.

Love to warm them and keep them safe through the bad times.

Was she hoping for too much to want that for herself? Probably.

Her parents were reminiscing again, the way they had been when she walked into the room. Very quietly, she slipped out. She figured she'd hardly be missed.

On a whim, instead of driving home, Caroline decided to stop by the high school. If she didn't miss her guess, Sloan would still be at rehearsal. He could probably use her help. Since his mother had had Joey and Danny overnight, Caroline felt it was a safe call to assume that Joan Walters would opt for a break. That meant Sloan had been forced to bring the boys with him. She'd be doing him a favor by volunteering to look after them. She liked doing things for him. Liked doing things with him and the boys. It was as close as she'd ever come to knowing what life would be like if she had a husband and children of her own.

She shook her head as she walked to the auditorium from the parking lot. If asked, she would have said that she had come to terms with that longing years ago. That she had substituted her profession for it. But that had been before she returned to Bedford. Before she had the opportunity to peer through a window at a life that might have been hers, had Sloan loved her instead of Julie.

This was no time to get maudlin, she told herself as she opened the auditorium door.

Music assailed her. She recognized it immediately. The orchestra was playing "Anything You Can Do, I Can Do Better." A sentiment she'd always lived by, she thought, amused.

The high pitched female voice, ever so slightly off-key, made her wince as it hit the wrong note.

That didn't sound like Allison.

Caroline slowly made her way toward the stage. It wasn't Allison who was singing, she realized. It was a girl she recognized from the chorus. The girl was standing in the foreground with Matt, obviously playing Annie. Where was Allison?

Joey and Danny, bored with playing with the prop six-shooters and pretending that they were cowboys, turned toward her at the same time. Their faces lit up. Within a beat, they were racing each other up the aisle, calling out her name.

Caroline placed her finger on her lips. "Shhh."

They clamped their lips together gleefully. Then, hooking their arms around her, they dragged Caroline down to their level.

"Where have you been? We haven't seen you since

forever,'' Danny moaned, nuzzling against her before he remembered that it wasn't a big-boy thing to do.

"Longer," Joey declared, raising his voice to outdo his brother.

"Shhh," she admonished again with a wink. "Your dad's trying to concentrate."

Her heart swelling, Caroline hugged both boys to her. She had to admit, she had really gotten hooked on this small-fry affection. It was addicting.

Almost as addicting as making love with Sloan.

She didn't want to think about doing without either until she had to. Right now, everything was perfect. She knew the danger of complacency and of getting caught up in too much happiness, but she couldn't help herself. It felt wonderful.

Sloan looked frustrated as he came over to her after the number was over. He'd told everyone to take five.

"What happened to your star?" Caroline asked.

He frowned. This was just what he needed. What had possessed him to ever agree to take on this headache? "She quit."

Caroline looked at him, still resting a hand on each boy's shoulder. "Quit?" Allison had seemed so caught up in the show. "When?"

"Today. She sent a note with one of her girlfriends, said she didn't think she was right for the part." Frustrated, Sloan shoved his hands into his pockets. "She was perfect for the part. Everything was going great. I don't know what's gotten into her."

Well, this just reinforced her suspicions, Caroline thought. "Guys, I need to talk to your dad." They looked up at her reluctantly, then nodded in unison. Caroline motioned Sloan to the rear. When they were out of earshot of the boys, she said, "I think that *was* Allison on the phone this morning. I think that when she heard my voice, she realized that you were seeing someone and that left her out in the cold. This is the only way she can get back at you.''

He wanted to say that she was letting her imagination run away with her, but he was beginning to think she was right. He ran his hand through his hair. ''I don't need this, Caroline.''

She knew he wouldn't walk away from the play, no matter how bad it got. He'd given his word, and he'd see the play through. ''But from the sound of it, you do need her. Want me to talk to her for you? Woman to woman?''

That wasn't the solution, though he appreciated the offer. ''If what you're saying is true, to Allison you are the *other* woman. I don't think you'll have much clout with her.''

She still wanted to try. ''Let me work that out.''

''No, I think I have an idea.'' One that had just occurred to him. ''Matt,'' Sloan called to the student, ''can I see you for a minute?''

Matt wasted no time in getting over to him. The teenager looked as unhappy about his new partner as Sloan was.

He had the decency to lower his voice as he registered his complaint. ''Man, it just isn't working between us, Mr. Walters. Jane's nice and all, but—''

For Jane's sake, Sloan refrained from heartily agreeing. Instead, he said, ''I think I have a way to get Allison back.''

Matt looked dubious. ''I don't know, Mr. Walters, lately she's been acting real weird.'' The teenager anticipated his suggestion. ''If you want me to talk to her, I don't think she'll listen. Maybe she'll listen to you—''

He didn't want to put himself in that position. The last thing Sloan needed was to be alone with Allison, trying to reason with her. Who knew what sort of fantasy she'd conjured up about the two of them in her mind?

What he proposed to do was to fight fantasy with a strong dose of reality. Reality, in this case, came in the guise of a young, handsome, *available* suitor. Matt.

"No, I think it's more important that she changes her mind about leaving the play because of something you said, not me." Draping his arm around the teenager's shoulders, Sloan took him aside and told Matt what he wanted him to do.

Caroline couldn't hear, but from the way the expression on Matt's face went from dubious to hopeful to pleased, she figured that whatever Sloan was saying, it was making points.

Joey tugged on her sleeve. "What are they talking about, Caroline?"

He sounded as if he felt left out, she thought. "Guy talk."

"Like about which team is winning and what they did to win?" Danny guessed.

In this case, it was easier agreeing than explaining. "Something like that."

"C'mon, Joey, let's talk guy talk." Danny hooked his thumbs in his belt and rocked on the balls of his feet. He sounded like a little old man when he asked, "Think the Angels'll be in the World Series this year?"

Joey, beneath the Angels cap his father wouldn't let him wear sideways, was the picture of confidence. "Sure," he lisped.

Caroline smothered a laugh. She could have eaten them both up in one bite.

Chapter 14

Caroline sat in Sloan's kitchen, nursing a cup of coffee. She'd just put up a fresh pot, though she didn't need the caffeine. Just being around Sloan energized her.

The table between them was littered with half-empty little white cartons of Chinese food. She vaguely gave some thought to cleaning up, then assuaged her conscience with the word, *later*. She didn't want anything detracting from the moment. Sloan had picked up the cartons on his way home, wanting to celebrate the triumphant execution of his plan. Allison had literally been wooed back to her role, and though he hadn't been the wooer, he took no small credit for the occurrence.

She loved seeing Sloan look so satisfied with himself. Even cocky looked good on him, she mused. She tried to remember a time when she hadn't loved him, and couldn't.

Caroline leaned her chin on her upturned palm. She

didn't have to pretend to be caught up in what he was telling her. "So then what happened?"

"Matt did exactly what I told him to do."

In the middle of his narrative, Sloan paused as he looked into Caroline's eyes. He could lose himself there. Probably had lost himself there. When had it happened? How? The exact steps were blurred. But it had happened. He didn't know whether to feel happy about it or afraid. Caring about someone wasn't as simple as it had once been.

He got back to his story. "Flowers, candy, a few golden words from a learned older man, and voilà," he said, snapping his fingers, "Allison sees Matt in a whole new light." He knotted his hands behind his head and leaned back in his chair, extremely pleased with himself. "As simple as that."

His leading lady back and, so far, no more strange phone calls at odd hours. No wonder he was feeling smug. "It usually is."

Sloan raised an eyebrow at what she'd left unsaid. "Meaning?"

Caroline shrugged carelessly. "People have a tendency to overanalyze things." Drinking the last of her coffee, she wrapped her hands around the cup. It still felt a little warm. "Sometimes things lose their allure if they're held under a microscope. Better just to go with the effect."

"Not always." His eyes were smiling at her as he reached for her hand. "If I held you under a microscope, I have a feeling I'd find exactly what I see now."

She laughed at the image. "First you'd have to find a very big microscope."

"I'd rather do the job myself." Gently he pulled her from her chair and onto his lap. "I've discovered that about some things, I'm a hands-on kind of guy.'' He tucked his around her waist.

She knew she would willingly remain like this until eternity ran out of grains of sand. ''How long did you say Joey and Danny would be gone?''

He thought a minute, as if he hadn't already calculated the time before he invited her over to celebrate. ''At least three hours. After the movie, the Cub Scout leader is taking them out for sodas. Twenty-three kids, all yelling at once.''

She winced in sympathy. ''Poor man.''

He didn't want to waste time talking about the Cub Scout leader. The man had known what he was getting into when he volunteered. Unlike him. Sloan hadn't had a clue what was waiting for him when he first kissed Caroline.

He nuzzled her now, inhaling the light fragrance he'd come to associate with her. Light or not, it still intoxicated him.

''Wouldn't want to think he made that huge sacrifice for nothing.'' Sloan nipped her lower lip, lightly flicking his tongue along it. She squirmed on his lap, a little moan escaping her lips. He grinned as his eyes darted up to hers. ''Why is it I can't seem to keep my hands off you?''

Regaining a little of her composure, she combed her fingers through his hair. She loved the thick feel of it as it brushed against her skin. ''You're analyzing again. I thought we agreed not to.''

She tried to sound playful, but she was dead serious. She was afraid that once he began to analyze his feelings, guilt would take him away from her. Caroline wasn't ready to give him up yet.

As if she would ever be ready, she thought, mocking herself.

"Sorry." He toyed with the ends of her hair, watching her eyes grow smoky. Enjoying the thrill that went through him. "Occupational habit. I see poetry, I want to analyze it."

She nestled closer. She doubted it was possible to be any happier than she was right now and still live. "Is that what I am? Poetry?"

"Sheer poetry." He was still smiling, but she could see that he had become serious.

She cocked her head, couching her question in a metaphor. It was safer that way. "Am I an ode or a limerick?"

Delighted, he kissed her again, a little more deeply, a little more passionately. At the last moment, he stopped himself from getting carried away.

Sloan laughed. "That's what I get for making love with a woman who got straight As in high school English."

"Straight As in everything," she reminded him haughtily.

He wasn't fooled. Caroline was the last person in the world to brag. The last to take anything for granted, especially the effect she had on him. He brushed his lips over hers again. He was teasing himself, as well as her. "An epic poem. How's that?"

The flames he was fanning were getting higher. Framing his face in her hands, she brought her mouth to his, giving him a dose of his own medicine.

"That'll do fine," she told him.

And if she didn't believe there was any truth in the playful banter, she could pretend. After all, pretending had gotten her this far. Pretending that he was serious.

Pretending that what was between them would last, when she knew it was all just emotions written on the wind. They would blow away the first time the breeze shifted. She'd done without him too long to believe that he was finally hers.

The urgency that took over his body and mind was one that he was becoming accustomed to. It seemed every time he was alone with Caroline it leaped out to possess him. And times when he wasn't alone with her, when the room was crowded with his sons and their boisterous noise, the urgency came then, too.

There was no getting away from it. He wanted her. Night and day. All the time.

Was it just the novelty of feeling again that prompted this? Or was it something more?

He didn't know.

Caroline skimmed her fingertips over his brow, smoothing it delicately. "You're doing it again."

Her words broke through his thoughts. "What?"

He knew perfectly well what. "Thinking. Analyzing."

His arms still around her, he tucked her closer against him. "You want me to stop thinking?"

There wasn't even a moment's hesitation. "Yes. Just feel, Sloan." She put everything she was feeling into the kiss she pressed to his lips. Her breath was hot against his skin as she repeated, "Just feel."

As he covered her with his hands, Caroline let the charge of heat coursing through her body take her away. Loving him was all that mattered for now. Later would somehow take care of itself.

At least she could pretend that it would.

Wanda looked up from the program she was watching. Beside her, her husband had fallen asleep on the sofa

She gently eased herself away from him and rose to follow Caroline to the front door.

"Wait, let me take a look at you."

Playing it up to the hilt, Caroline held out her hands like a stiff doll and then slowly turned around. The form-fitting red dress clung to her as she moved.

She supposed she owed this to her mother. Wanda Masters was an incurable romantic who had wanted to vicariously relive her own youth through her daughter. Up until now, there had been nothing to relive with. All through high school, the only dates Caroline had had involved study groups.

"You look lovely, dear." Wanda looked at her knowingly. "And I won't wait up, I promise."

The remark surprised Caroline. In her own way, her mother was saying that if she wanted to stay overnight at Sloan's, it was all right with her. When had she gotten so liberal-minded?

"Mother, I'm just going to see a high school play. This is a PG date."

Date. There, she'd said it. She was dating Sloan Walters. Seventeen years behind schedule, but it was finally happening.

Wanda was unconvinced. The fantasy she'd spun in her head was very convincing, as well as very satisfying. It involved Caroline and a roomful of grandchildren. "Still, things have a way of happening."

This was her mother? Caroline was tempted to ask to see some identification.

"His sons are going to be with me. And then we're all going to a cast party, after which we'll come back to his place. With the boys," she added emphatically. Neither one of them wanted to take a chance on being "discovered" by either Joey or Danny.

Wanda was unfazed. "Children sleep."

Caroline laughed as she impulsively hugged her mother. "I can't believe I'm having this conversation with you. You were always so very straitlaced when it came to sex." Even when it came to the crucial "mother-daughter" talk, Wanda had nervously handed her several pamphlets and said that she could arrange an appointment with Dr. Wiseman if Caroline had any questions about what she read.

"Love," Wanda corrected. Picking it up from the hall table, she handed Caroline her purse. "There's a difference."

"Yes, I know." And she was infinitely glad that her mother did, too.

It wasn't always easy, making herself understood, but Wanda tried. "And maybe nearly losing your father has loosened me up a little." There was a silent entreaty in her eyes as she looked at Caroline. "I want to enjoy every minute we have together. And I want you to enjoy yourself, too."

"I am, Mother. Maybe for the first time in my life, I am," she allowed.

Wanda nodded. "I thought as much." She saw questions rising in Caroline's eyes. "Don't you think I knew that you were in love with Sloan?"

Even now, it was second nature for her to deny it. She'd done it for so long, to protect everyone concerned. "I never said anything."

As if words were really necessary. "You didn't have to. It was there, in your eyes. It broke my heart when he married someone else."

Caroline found that difficult to believe. If it was true,

why had her mother never made one attempt to comfort her? "You never said anything."

Shame tinted her cheeks. She should have tried, Wanda thought. But it had been easier just pretending not to know.

"I didn't know what to say," she admitted helplessly. "Not every mother is blessed with the ability to know just the right words to utter. I'm afraid you got short-changed there, Caro."

Moved, Caroline hugged her mother again. "I never thought so." She had to leave before she became misty. She had yet to find mascara that lived up to its claim of being waterproof. The last thing she needed was to turn into a raccoon. "Well, I'd better get going before Sloan thinks I've forgotten about him. His car picked this morning to die, so I'm picking him and the boys up before the play." She gave her mother a quick kiss. "See you later."

"Have fun," Wanda called after her.

"That goes without saying. She's going to see Sloan."

Surprised, Wanda turned away from the door, shutting it in her wake. She looked at her husband. "I thought you were asleep. Were you listening the whole time?"

He merely smiled, reminding her of the young man who had walked into her life over thirty-five years ago. "A man can learn a lot of things by pretending to be asleep."

"You old dog."

He laughed, pulling her down beside him. "Not so old, Wanda. Not so old. Right now, I'm feeling very young again."

Wanda leaned into his kiss.

* * *

Who would ever have thought that her mother would be pushing her into Sloan's arms? Caroline mused as she pulled out of the driveway.

Not that she needed to be pushed. Not anymore. The uncertainty that had always held her back had been taken away. He wanted her. She could see it in his eyes, feel it in his touch. As for love, well, that was something to be worked out later.

For now, everything was going well. Almost too well. Her father was recovering more quickly than originally anticipated; her plans to relocate had been finalized with the fortuitous purchase of Dr. Brady's practice—she was targeting the first of August to open her doors—and things between her and Sloan couldn't be more perfect.

So perfect that it almost made her nervous.

She squelched the thought. She wasn't going to think about the future; she was only going to concentrate on the present. A present that was far richer than she'd ever dreamed possible. In the past two weeks, ever since they'd made love that first time after the party, Sloan had made the most of their moments alone. And she loved being with the boys almost as much as she loved being with Sloan.

Things, she felt sure, just didn't get any better than this.

So why, amid all this happiness, was there this odd premonition spiking through her? Why did she have to ruin it for herself by worrying that somewhere there was a second shoe waiting to drop?

"You're just too damn serious for your own good, Caroline," she muttered under her breath as she turned down Sloan's street.

* * *

Sloan looked at his watch. There was less than half an hour before he was supposed to be at the auditorium. Caroline would be here before then. And he still hadn't found his black shoes.

Served him right for not laying everything out, the way he'd intended.

The road to hell... he thought in exasperation, getting off his knees. They weren't under the coffee table, the way he'd hoped. He'd run out of ideas.

"Guys," he called out, "have either of you seen my black shoes?"

"Yeah," Danny's voice piped up. Squirming in clothes he hated, Danny walked into the living room. "Lots of times."

Hope crashed and burned. He should have known. "I mean lately." Clenched fists on hips, Sloan turned toward his older son. "Like today."

Danny shook his head. "Uh-uh." Like a child in a grade B movie, he stuck his finger in his collar and tried to pull the fabric away from his neck. "Do I gotta wear this, Dad?"

He was in no mood for a fashion discussion. Or rebellion.

"Yes, you 'gotta.' It won't kill you to look presentable, just this once." He opened the hall closet. A basketball rolled out. No shoes. Where could they have gotten to? "Joey, have you been playing with my shoes again?"

"Nope." Joey, looking as uncomfortable as his brother, straggled into the room. Why did he have to wear a dopey old suit, anyway? What was wrong with his jeans and his favorite T-shirt? The chocolate ice cream streaks were almost gone.

Sloan bit back his temper. One of them had probably

made off with his shoes to play dress-up in and forgotten about it. They were always doing things like that.

"Well, I can't go barefoot," he declared to no one in particular. His brown shoes didn't go with what he'd chosen to wear, and it was too late to change.

"You can have my boots," Joey offered. Maybe if he gave Dad his boots, Dad would let him wear his jeans.

"They're too small," Sloan answered absently.

He sighed. Damn it, anyway. He'd been through the whole house, without any luck. They had to be here somewhere. There was nothing to do but start at the beginning again. Grumbling, looking at his watch again, Sloan headed for the stairs.

The bed, he realized—he hadn't looked under his bed. Maybe he'd inadvertently kicked them under there...

Right. The last time he made love with Caroline, he'd had his black shoes on, he remembered.

With renewed hope and mumbling half a prayer, he sprinted up the stairs two at a time just as the doorbell rang.

"I'll get it!" Joey cried, pivoting on his heel.

Danny tried to get ahead of him. "No, I'm the older one."

"Ask who it is first," Sloan reminded them, disappearing into his bedroom.

"It's gotta be Caroline," Joey insisted excitedly. "She said she was coming to take us."

Danny looked down his nose at his brother. "Always ask," he cautioned importantly.

Deftly, he avoided Joey's cast as the latter swung it in his direction. His brother had gotten good at wheedling the cast like a weapon, but he'd learned how to move out of the way quickly.

Though there was no way he could see through the

peephole, Danny stood on his toes and pretended to look out.

"Who is it?" he cried.

His hand clamped on to the doorknob before Joey had a chance to claim it. Joey pouted.

On the other side, Caroline smiled to herself. She'd seen the tug-of-war between them often enough to be able to envision it.

"It's Caroline." The door swung open immediately. Two very uncomfortable-looking boys greeted her simultaneously. Caroline covered her heart. "My, who are these handsome hunks? I was looking for Joey and Danny Walters."

Joey looked puzzled. "Don'tcha recognize us, Caroline? It's us." He jerked a thumb at himself. "Joey and Danny."

"She knows that, dork." Danny poked him. "She's just teasing." His eyes shifted to Caroline, looking for confirmation. "Right?"

She chose her words carefully. "Maybe a little, but you guys do look very handsome." Leaning over, she adjusted Danny's tie. He was wearing it askew. "I'd say blue is your color, Dan."

Dan. Danny beamed. He liked the way that sounded, like he was all grown up.

Caroline looked around. She'd expected Sloan to be right at the door, ready to go. Both of them hated being late.

"So, where's the director?" Danny looked at her, a little uncertain. "Your dad?" she added, prompting him.

"Oh!" The light dawned. "He's upstairs. Looking for his shoes."

He wasn't ready? "Uh-oh." Caroline winked at the two boys. "Sounds like your dad could use my help.

Never knew a man yet who could find what he was looking for under pressure.''

Her faithful companions danced about eagerly at her side. "Can we help?" Danny asked.

"Yeah, can we?"

They'd only get in the way, and Sloan was probably tense enough as it was. She turned down the offer as diplomatically as she could.

"No, you guys stay down here and just look gorgeous. Wouldn't want to see either of you getting your clothes wrinkled."

Leaving them sitting in the living room, Caroline hurried up the stairs. "Sloan? Where are you? Danny said you were looking for your shoes. Have you found them yet?"

His back was to her when she entered his room. He was sitting on the bed, probably descending into despair, she thought. It had to be a guy thing, Caroline decided. Her father could never find anything, either.

"Don't worry, the cavalry is here. Do you by any chance remember when you—"

She stopped when she saw the expression on his face. Sloan looked devastated, as if his entire world had just collapsed on him.

He looked exactly the way he had the day he took the call from the police telling him that Julie had been killed.

Caroline's heart sank. This wasn't about looking for a pair of shoes. Something was very wrong.

"Sloan, what is it? What's the matter?"

Everything. How could he ever have thought that he could feel again?

Sloan took a deep breath. Emotion choked him. For a minute, he couldn't even talk. All he could do was look at the slipper he was clutching.

Julie's slipper.

It brought everything back to him. Everything he'd been trying so hard to deny, to bury. The pain, the loss. The rage. All the emotions that he'd never let out, that he'd thought he'd conquered, were now threatening to conquer him.

He spoke slowly, in a disembodied voice. "I was looking under the bed for my shoes. And I found this. I guess they forgot to take it."

She could feel her chest constricting. "They?" she whispered.

"Her mother and sisters." He couldn't even bring himself to say her name. "I had them clear her things out. Everything. It all went to charity." He struggled. When he spoke again, his voice was dead, devoid of feeling. "After all, it wasn't as if anyone here was going to use any of it." Sloan pressed his lips together. "They missed this."

He cursed as he felt a tear slide down. Damn it, anyway. Why couldn't he control himself?

She saw the tear, and ached for him. Ached for herself. Somewhere in the distance, Caroline could have sworn she heard the other shoe drop.

Chapter 15

Caroline put her hand on his shoulder in silent comfort. She felt his shoulder stiffen defensively. Sloan was still keeping it all bottled up, the torment, the grief.

For a moment, she wanted to retreat. But that would be only thinking of herself, not of him. And he was the one who needed help.

"Sloan, it's all right to grieve, to hurt. It's only natural. It's part of the healing process."

His face was impassive, rigid. So tense it looked as if his bones were made of steel. Caroline could almost see him blocking the onslaught of emotion that, for one moment, had almost overwhelmed him. "Oh, Sloan, you have to let it out," she begged him.

If you don't, love can't come in. There's no room for it.

She went to embrace him, but he shrugged her away, rising. If she hugged him, he knew, the tears would come. He wouldn't be able to stop them. So he did the only thing he could to survive. He shrugged her away. He couldn't break down.

Couldn't let her in.

Sloan couldn't have hurt her any more if he deliberately tried.

"We'll be late," he said stonily.

As he walked out of the room, he dropped the slipper in the wastepaper basket.

The sound reverberated in her head. *The other shoe,* she thought cryptically, staring at the heel that peeked out of the basket. *Who would ever have thought it would be a slipper?*

Caroline felt numb.

The next moment, she was surrounded by Joey and Danny, who were running around her like puppies chasing their tails. They'd come to get her.

"Aren't you coming, Caroline?" Joey asked.

"'Course she's coming. She's gotta come. She's the driver," Danny told him, with the superior air of one who knew everything. But the look he gave Caroline was uncertain.

She rallied. She had no choice. There was no way she was going to drag them into this. They'd know soon enough, anyway.

Caroline draped an arm around each set of small shoulders, swallowing the hot tears that had threatened to spill out. She didn't want to let them see her crying. "Okay, guys, let's go see a play."

The short ride to the high school would have been uncomfortably quiet if Danny and Joey hadn't been with them. The brothers had found yet another thing to argue about. Their voices swelled in the back seat as the argument escalated.

Caroline was grateful for the distracting noise. She wouldn't have been able to stand it otherwise. Sloan sat next to her in withdrawn silence. She could feel his pain, yet there wasn't a thing she could do about it. He wouldn't let her even try.

All she could think of was that he was shutting her out. Would always shut her out.

He needed time to get his head together, Sloan thought, but he didn't have it. What he did have was thirty nervous students—thirty-nine, if he counted the orchestra—waiting for him to lend them moral support.

Just as well. He really didn't want to think; he just wanted to salvage control over himself. To become numb again, and not feel anything. The way he'd been doing before Caroline returned. Somehow, she had crept into his life and dismantled the protective shields around him. The shields that had helped him survive this last year.

For the first time in his life, Sloan wished he drank, really drank. Alcohol would have easily anesthetized this feeling crowding him, slicing away at him from all angles.

As he got out of the car, Sloan looked at Caroline. He didn't mean to take it out on her. But if it hadn't been for her…

"I've got to go backstage. Boys, go with Caroline. I'll see you after the play." His eyes shifted fleetingly toward Caroline. "I'm sorry." And then he turned his back on her as he hurried off.

She watched him disappear around the corner of the building. "So am I," she said quietly.

"What's Dad sorry about, Caroline?" Joey wanted to know.

"He's sorry he can't sit with us during the play." The

excuse came automatically to her lips, by the grace of some part of her that had gone into survival mode.

"Why can't he sit with us?" Joey pressed as they walked to the front entrance.

"He's going to be busy backstage."

"Can we be busy backstage, too?" Danny hung on her arm. "We know everybody back there."

She handed their tickets to a girl standing by the door and shepherded the boys inside. "You've got a more important job to do. You're the cheering section."

"Should we rehearse?" Danny asked, remembering that was what his father had said actors do.

Caroline found their seats in the first row. "You'll be fine. You're both naturals."

The questions they continued to shower her with kept her mind occupied. But her heart was another matter. It felt as if it were breaking in half.

It didn't help, looking at Joey and Danny, knowing that this would be the last time she was with them.

Sloan let out a long breath. Two hours and fifteen minutes was a long time to be holding it. That was how long the performance ran. It had gone a little over their dress rehearsal time. At the last minute, they'd misplaced the peace pipe for "Annie's" induction-to-the-tribe number and had to make a substitution. But all in all, the performance had gone far better than he hoped. Allison and Matt had played brilliantly off each other. Sparks had turned to romance, and the audience had gone along for the ride, enjoying themselves immensely. There were seven curtain calls in all.

At the final one, Allison came forward, a beautiful bouquet of long-stemmed yellow roses from Matt cradled in her arms. Quieting the applause, although not too quickly, she gave a little speech, saying how the play would have been a total disaster if not for Sloan's efforts and guidance.

The audience, by its renewed applause, showed their appreciation for this minor miracle.

Sloan caught the eye of the assistant principal and figured that had put the final nail in his coffin. There was no getting out of being next year's director, unless he moved away. He found himself not completely put off by the thought of tackling a new play.

Someone in the wings hurried up to give Allison a plaque, which she in turn presented to Sloan.

"This is just a small token of our appreciation. We all chipped in for it. 'To Mr. Walters,'" she read. "'A good director, a great teacher and an even better friend.'" Allison brushed her lips lightly across Sloan's cheek as she presented him with the plaque. "Thanks for setting me straight," she whispered, then retreated to stand beside Matt.

One glance at them told Sloan that he didn't have to worry about late-night phone calls anymore.

"I'd like to thank each one of the cast for giving me a very special experience I won't forget anytime soon. Now, everyone's invited backstage for cake." He beckoned the audience forward.

"Does that mean us, too, Caroline?" Joey wanted to know. "Or do we still gotta sit here and cheer?" His little feet were practically twitching.

"That means you, too," she said fondly. "Just don't knock down anyone in your hurry."

She doubted either one of the boys really heard the last part as they dashed up the steps on the side of the stage.

She took her time in joining them.

When she did, she hung back the way she used to, taking it all in. A long table borrowed from the cafeteria held a cornucopia of food brought in by various members of the cast and crew. Half the cast were milling around it. Energy was running high in the aftermath of their triumphant performance. Several of the girls were doting on Joey and Danny, loading their plates with different kinds of cakes and cookies.

Neither boy was protesting, Caroline noted with a smile.

She looked around for Sloan. He was standing off to one side, surrounded by parents and teachers. Everyone was congratulating him on what he had managed to accomplish on a shoestring. He looked as if he were enjoying himself. She was glad for him.

Caroline was careful not to make eye contact.

"You look sad, Caroline. Didn't you get some cake yet?" Joey asked. He held up his plate to her for examination.

His mouth was so stuffed, he looked like a squirrel storing nuts for the winter. She wondered how he managed to talk.

"No, I didn't," she answered, then shook her head when he offered to share some from his plate. "I'm not really hungry, thank you."

"But it's chocolate. You sick, Caroline?" Danny stopped eating. His face puckered in concern as he looked up at her.

She forced a smile. "No, I'm fine, honey, but thanks for asking."

But she wasn't fine. She wasn't fine at all, because she knew that it was over. Over before it had really had a chance to begin. She just had to find enough strength to finally close the door.

* * *

With the play now behind him, Sloan felt better. And guilty about the way he'd behaved toward Caroline earlier. Maybe there was some way he could make amends. He knew he wanted to try.

"Why don't you come in for some coffee?" he urged Caroline as they approached his house. With the boys bedded down, they could talk. He knew he didn't have it in him to give what Caroline needed, but he did want them to remain friends.

Caroline shook her head. She didn't want to prolong this any more than necessary. Pulling up the hand brake, she kept the engine running. "No, it's late, I'd better be going."

He didn't want her to leave. There was a strange note in her voice, a note that made him feel uneasy. He didn't want her to go until he was sure it was all right between them.

"Wait here, I just want to unlock the door for the boys." Holding the car door open, he motioned Joey and Danny out. It was hours past their bedtime, and they looked almost subdued.

She didn't want to wait. She needed to leave, before he saw her cry. "No, I'm going to—"

He wasn't about to argue about this. "Wait here," he said again, firmly.

Against her better judgment, she waited, the imprint of each boy's good-night kiss throbbing on her cheek. That only added to her pain.

Sloan ushered the boys into the house, flipping on the hall light. "Get ready for bed. I'll be up in a few minutes." He waited until they began to straggle up the stairs, for once too tired to argue about being sent to bed.

He hurried back to the car, afraid that Caroline would drive away if he took too long.

By the expression on her face as he got in, he knew she'd been thinking about it. The engine was still running.

"Look, I'm sorry if I ignored you at the party," he began, stumbling into his apology. "But there were just so many—"

She cut him off. "I'm not upset about that. I'm glad they gave you some of the appreciation you deserved. It was a great performance."

He didn't give a damn about the performance right now. What he cared about was that there was something wrong between them and he really wasn't sure how to fix it. Or what to say. He hadn't had a chance to talk to her during the party, and there'd been no opportunity on the ride home, with the boys in the back seat.

The question, now that he had a chance to ask, came cautiously. "Then what are you upset about?" Once she put it into words, maybe they could work from there.

Since he'd asked, he obviously didn't know. Didn't understand. And probably never would. "Earlier," she answered honestly, "in your bedroom."

He'd tried desperately to pull back before his emotions could get the better of him. Before he made a fool of himself in front of her. It had nothing to do with her. "What did I say?"

No, he truly didn't know, she thought, and that made it hurt even more.

"Nothing." She turned in her seat and faced him squarely. "You said nothing. That's just it. You said nothing, and pushed me away."

He was trying to protect her from the scene. And protect himself, as well. "I said nothing because there's nothing to say."

Did he really believe that? She thought of just giving up, of asking him to get out of the car and driving away, but that was the coward's way out, and she wasn't a coward. Not anymore.

"There's plenty to say, Sloan. You're hurting."

It was a side of him that he didn't want her to see. "I don't want to share my pain with you, Caroline. I want to share laughter, good times." That was what he needed her for. To brighten his world.

Didn't he understand that wasn't enough? "It's no good that way, Sloan. I want to share your pain as well as your laughter. I want to share *everything*. It's all or nothing." She let out a shaky sigh. "And since it can't be all, I guess it's nothing."

Caroline released the hand brake, easing her foot onto the brake pedal. She was fighting tears, hoping she could get through this without crying. The words came out slowly. "I don't think we should see each other for a while, Sloan."

He stared at her, feeling as if someone had just punched him. "You don't mean that."

"Yes, I do." Who would ever have thought? It almost seemed perversely funny to her. "I never thought I'd hear myself say I didn't want to see you, but I don't." Caroline stared straight ahead, afraid that if she looked at him, she would break down. This had to be done, had to be said. "This is too painful for me. Maybe things happened too fast. Maybe they were happening for the wrong reason, I don't know. All I know is that I can't stand by, seeing you, wanting you, and knowing that I can't have you. I want children, Sloan. And a husband who can share his heart with me. I can't have that wi you." Tears burned her eyes. She blinked them back. "You'd better go see about the boys. They'll be wondering where you are."

Because he didn't know what else to do, he got out. But as the car began to back away, he called after her. "Caroline—"

"I'll see you around, Sloan." *But not too soon.* Caroline drove away before she could change her mind and rush back.

Angry, confused, without a target to focus on, Sloan walked into the house. He managed to hold himself together and tuck Joey and Danny into bed, answering their sleepy questions without really hearing them or knowing what he said in reply.

He went into his bedroom and closed the door behind him, wanting to slam it. Wanting to throw something against the wall and watch it smash into a million pieces, the way he felt his life was being smashed.

For just a moment, he considered it, looking around for something to throw. He needed to vent the huge wave of anger that was rising within his chest like the mother of all tidal waves. He knew he couldn't. It would scare Joey and Danny.

He couldn't swallow the anger. It was choking him so that he couldn't breathe.

He was angry at Caroline for asking things of him that he couldn't give. Angry at himself for losing control like that in front of her. Men didn't cry, they didn't fall apart. At least he didn't.

Most of all, Sloan realized, he was angry at Julie, for dying. For leaving him.

The thought assailed him, slapping him in the face. That was it. That was what he'd been denying for so long. He was angry, angry at Julie. So angry that it was ripping him up inside.

But it wasn't her fault. It wasn't anyone's fault except the driver of the other car, and he had died in the crash that took Julie's life.

Sloan had no target.

Very slowly, like a man trapped within a dream in which he was doomed to move about in slow motion, Sloan walked over to the wastepaper basket. Bending over it, he took out the slipper he'd thrown away.

Sloan closed his eyes, holding the slipper to him and remembering.

And then he cried.

Each day, the emptiness within threatened to eat her up alive.

Caroline tackled it the only way she knew how. By filling it. Filling it with everything imaginable. She immersed herself in all kinds of things, keeping so busy that she had no time to think, or even to string two breaths together in succession.

There was no shortage of demands on her time. The morning after the play, she took over her father's rehab program, throwing herself into it even more than she had before. She worked with him when the therapist wasn't there. She spent time with her mother, showing her how to take care of things that needing doing. Simple things that had eluded her previously.

Bringing her into the nineties, Caroline thought with a smile. At least she was accomplishing something.

In what time there was left, she turned her attention to the practice she was to open soon. There were nurses to interview, equipment to get, new furniture to buy, even paint and carpeting to consider. The old office decor didn't generate the proper atmosphere for children. They needed to feel that this was a safe place for them, a place they weren't afraid to come to.

Caroline saw to it that there wasn't a moment left in the day when she could let herself think about Sloan.

That left only her dreams.

She saw his face in her dreams a dozen times a night. She could block her thoughts during the day, but there was no escaping them when she was asleep.

So she slept less. Eventually, she knew, she would get over him.

In a hundred years or so.

As the office began to take shape, she found herself becoming heartened. After all, this was her dream. Being a pediatrician was all she had ever wanted to be.

That, and Sloan's wife.

One out of two wasn't bad, she thought as she walked into her office.

It was just a little after ten o'clock. Her mother had insisted on working with her father today, after the therapist finished. That had left Caroline with nothing to do. Resting was out of the question. She didn't want to have time on her hands. So, she'd come here. There were pamphlets on computers she could review. Getting a new one was essential.

The smell of fresh paint greeted her immediately. The job was going more slowly than she'd anticipated, but the painter she'd hired preferred working alone.

"That way," he'd claimed when she accepted his bid, "I know the job'll be done right." He was egotistical, but he was good and he came recommended.

He also came late.

Where was he? she wondered, looking around. Caroline picked her way to the back office, careful not to trip over the drop cloths that seemed to be everywhere.

"Ramon?" She peered into one of the examining rooms. He had yet to start here, she noted. "Where are you?"

When she glimpsed the back of a man's head in the third examining room, she let out a sigh. "Why aren't you wearing coveralls?"

He turned around. "I will if you want me to."

"Sloan." Caroline's heart leaped up, only to come down with a resounding thud. Emotion gave way to logic, just this once. "What are you doing here? I thought we agreed not to see each other anymore."

He crossed to her. It had taken a lot for him to come here. A lot of soul-searching. Emptiness had tipped the scales. He hadn't been aware that the emptiness had left him until it returned again.

Caroline was the one who'd made it go away. He wanted her back in his life. In all their lives, he amended, thinking of his sons.

"You agreed," he pointed out, fighting the urge to sweep her into his arms and kiss her. They had to talk first. "As I remember, I had very little to do with that conversation."

Caroline took a step back, afraid that any second she was going to throw her arms round his neck, ready to accept any terms. Neither of them would be happy that way.

She looked around nervously. She needed someone else around to keep her from doing something stupid. "Where's Ramon? The painter?" she added when he looked at her blankly.

"Oh, him. I sent him out for a break." He glanced at his watch. The man had left fifteen minutes ago. "We don't have much time." Unable to help himself, he gave in and drew her to him. It felt like heaven, holding her. "I've missed you."

God, but it felt good having him hold her. She tried valiantly not to sink into the sensation. With an effort, she braced her hands on his forearms, holding back.

"And I've missed you. So much so that I can hardly stand it." She was stronger, she realized, than she'd ever thought possible. "But I can't go back to what we were. We can't just drift along."

"I know that."

But she was willing, she thought, knowing it did no good to lie to herself. Willing just to drift, as long as the current took her along with him.

So much for backbone, she thought.

He read the hesitation in her eyes. Releasing her, he eased her into a chair.

"We need to talk. Actually, *I* need to talk—you need to listen." Taking a breath, Sloan plunged into the speech he'd been rehearsing ever since he made up his mind, last night. "I've done a lot of soul-searching since you left. You were right about my grief. I hadn't let it out. I think I've probably been running from it ever since Julie died." Just saying that took effort. But he was making progress.

Sloan laughed shortly. "No probably about it, I have been. If I didn't think, I didn't feel, and if I didn't feel, I didn't break down. I've hardly even said her name this last year."

He tried to make her understand why he'd done what he did. "Julie's dying was the most devastating thing that ever happened to me. Someone I loved died. I couldn't protect her, couldn't prevent it from happening. That scared the hell out of me. And then, you came into my life. Suddenly, I could laugh again. And slowly, I began to feel again.''

He wondered if she understood what she'd come to mean to him. And how she'd saved his life.

''The last thing on my mind when I ran into you in the supermarket that day was falling in love again. I didn't think it was possible for me. But obviously, I didn't know myself very well.'' A smile played on his lips. ''Almost as little as I knew you.

''But I am in love with you, Caroline. If I didn't consciously know it then, I do now. These last two weeks without you have been pure hell.'' His smile deepened. ''Not just because Joey and Danny are on my case because they think I did something to make you go away, but because you weren't there to talk to, weren't there to relax with. Weren't there when I turned in bed and reached for you.'' Kneeling before her, he took her hands in his. ''I want you there, Caroline. I want you in my life for as long as I can have you. I know it's not forever. I've finally accepted that death is a part of life. But I'll settle for what I can get.''

He searched her face, looking for a sign that he hadn't lost her.

''So what do you think? Do you love me enough to put up with me?'' Dropping her hands, he rose and dragged his hand through his hair. Talk about an egoist, he thought. He took the cake. ''Here I am assuming that you love me. Maybe you don't. Maybe—''

''Can I talk now?'' she asked.

He laughed, tension ricocheting through him. ''Yes, you can talk now.''

Caroline rose to face him. ''Good, because I have a lot to say. Number one, if you haven't figured out that I love you yet, then maybe you're not as smart as I always thought you were.'' She held up a second finger. ''Number two, we do have forever, because no matter what happens, I'll always love you, in this world or any other. And,'' she finished, a third finger joining the others, ''number three, do I love you enough to put up with you? Don't you know by now? I always have. I have loved you, Sloan Walters, ever since you walked into my second-period English class, dressed in black chinos, a black pullover and a disinterested frown.''

He stared at her, dumbfounded. ''You can remember that far back?''

She supposed that he would always be dense in some ways. ''I can remember everything about you at any given point in time.''

Her answer took him by surprise. She'd loved him for that long? How had he ever managed to be so blind? ''I never knew—''

She smiled at him fondly. ''You weren't supposed to. Julie was my best friend, and she was crazy about you. And you were nuts about her. Everyone knew that.''

It was all clear to him now. How could he have been so dense? ''That crush you told me you had on the guy who was already taken—was it me?''

''It was you.''

He didn't know what to say. ''Caroline, if I had only know—''

She wouldn't let him finish. There was no point to it. And no point to regrets. ''No ifs, Sloan. Just the facts.'' She looked up into his eyes. ''And the fact is, we have today.''

He took her into his arms. The emptiness was gone again. She'd made it go away. She always would. How did one man get to be so lucky, not once but twice?

"And all the tomorrows you want. Marry me, Caroline, be the mother of my children. All my children."

She raised a brow. "There're more?"

His smile was wicked as he pressed a kiss to her forehead. "There will be, as soon as we can leave here and get started." He feathered a kiss on her lips. "What do you say?"

She threw her arms around his neck. "Yes. Yes to everything."

He exhaled dramatically. "Thank God. Danny and Joey weren't going to let me back in the house unless I brought you with me."

Her heart was so full, she thought it would burst. "I always did like those boys."

"We'll have more," he promised her, bringing his mouth to hers.

"Count on it."

They sealed the bargain, and their fates, with a very long kiss.

* * * * *

DIANA PALMER
ANN MAJOR
SUSAN MALLERY

MONTANA MAVERICKS Weddings

RETURN TO WHITEHORN

In **April 1998** get ready to catch the bouquet. Join in the excitement as these bestselling authors lead us down the aisle with three heartwarming tales of love and matrimony in Big Sky country.

A very engaged lady is having second thoughts about her intended; a pregnant librarian is wooed by the town bad boy; a cowgirl meets up with her first love. Which Maverick will be the next one to get hitched?

Available in **April 1998.**

Silhouette's beloved **MONTANA MAVERICKS** returns in Special Edition and Harlequin Historicals starting in February 1998, with brand-new stories from your favorite authors.

Round up these great new stories at your favorite retail outlet.

Take 4 bestselling love stories FREE

Plus get a FREE surprise gift!

ALICIA SCOTT

Continues the twelve-book series— 36 Hours—in March 1998 with Book Nine

PARTNERS IN CRIME

The storm was over, and Detective Jack Stryker finally had a prime suspect in Grand Springs' high-profile murder case. But beautiful Josie Reynolds wasn't about to admit to the crime— nor did Jack want her to. He believed in her innocence, and he teamed up with the alluring suspect to prove it. But was he playing it by the book—or merely blinded by love?

For Jack and Josie and *all* the residents of Grand Springs, Colorado, the storm-induced blackout was just the beginning of 36 Hours that changed *everything!* You won't want to miss a single book.

Available at your favorite retail outlet.

FIVE STARS
MEAN SUCCESS

If you see the "5 Star Club" flash on a book, it means we're introducing you to one of our most STELLAR authors!

Every one of our Harlequin and Silhouette authors who has sold over 5 MILLION BOOKS has been selected for our "5 Star Club."

We've created the club so you won't miss any of our bestsellers. So, each month we'll be highlighting every original book within Harlequin and Silhouette written by our bestselling authors.

NOW THERE'S NO WAY ON EARTH OUR STARS WON'T BE SEEN!

OVER
5 MILLION
BOOKS SOLD
SPECIAL OFFER INSIDE

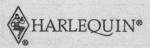

HARLEQUIN®   Silhouette®

P5STAR

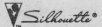